Destination:
Maui

Destination:
Maui

A Destination Murder Mystery

Ann Shepphird

4 Horsemen
Publications, Inc.

Destination: Maui
Destination Murder Mysteries Book 1
Copyright © 2021 Ann Shepphird. All rights reserved.

4 Horsemen
Publications, Inc.

4 Horsemen Publications, Inc.
1497 Main St. Suite 169
Dunedin, FL 34698
4horsemenpublications.com
info@4horsemenpublications.com

Typesetting by MC
Editor Jen Paquette

Library of Congress Control Number: 2021948562

Print ISBN: 978-1-64450-432-1
Audio ISBN: 978-1-64450-430-7
eBook ISBN: 978-1-64450-431-4

Thank you to all who helped bring this book to life, especially my partner, Jeff Wolf, who first inspired the notion of a series involving a mystery-solving travel writer. Years ago, while on a press trip that included a train ride from NYC to Montreal, I called him from the Algonquin Hotel and told him that one of the other writers on the trip was particularly difficult. From his response — "So, if there's a murder on the train, we know who it will be" — the idea was born.

Additional thanks go out to the friends and family who read the various versions of the manuscript and have encouraged me along the way, especially Amy Akiona, Jill Bastian, Lisa Furfine, John Shepphird, Jordan Weiner, and Jane Woodson.

Finally, I would like to dedicate this book to my beloved aunt, Ann Reynolds, whose belief in the project meant the world to me.

CHAPTER ONE

ppearances, as they say, can be deceiving. I had learned this more than once in my ten years as a crime reporter in Los Angeles. I was coming to understand the concept again after returning to my hometown of Carmel-by-the-Sea, California, and taking a new job as the travel columnist for *Carmel Today* magazine. And I was about to discover it yet again when someone turned out to be a murderer on my first press trip to a luxury resort on the Hawaiian island of Maui.

I realize there's a lot to unpack. Yes, I'm starting with a travel pun, but I really had been doing a lot of unpacking lately, both physically and mentally. I guess that's what happens when you don't expect to return home and make a career transition at the ripe old age of 34, huh?

Let me explain: My name is Samantha Powers—but everybody calls me Sam—and I returned to Carmel when I got the call from my Uncle Henry that my dad was diagnosed with Alzheimer's-related dementia and psychosis. Talk about your appearances: The diagnosis was something seemingly no one had seen coming, and yet the truth is the clues had been there for a while for anyone really paying attention.

It wasn't just that the clues were somewhat subtle; it's that no one—especially me, who had avoided visiting or, really, even calling very often after the death of my mom a decade earlier—had taken the time to put them together. The thing is— my dad would have put them together. Solving mysteries—criminal and otherwise—was something he did better than anyone I knew.

But not the rest of us. I mean, we maybe should have figured it out when Uncle Henry told me that my dad had been waking him up at 3 o'clock in the morning to discuss the crossword and adjusting the thermostat in the family home the two brothers shared to abnormal temperatures. Or when my dad called to wish me a happy birthday a month early and then spent a good 15 minutes arguing with me over the date. There had also been reports of him being spotted wandering all over town, but as the former police chief, that wasn't completely out of the ordinary either.

We all chalked these new and strange occurrences up to his ongoing grief after losing my mom and his retirement from the force. And since I was more than 300 miles away and the two of us had always had a somewhat prickly relationship on the best of days, I will admit I brushed a lot of it off. Maybe I wanted to. Maybe I was dealing with my own messes (spoiler alert: I was) and a little nervous he would put the clues together that my life wasn't exactly as it seemed.

Then, one day, Uncle Henry couldn't reach my dad from his office at the Monterey School of Law. He rushed home and found him lying on the bathroom floor talking to invisible people. That's when I got the call that I should drop the seemingly successful life I had built in Los Angeles and come home, at least temporarily, to help Uncle Henry handle it all.

My first month home was kind of a blur. At least it was a scenic blur from our home looking out over Carmel River State Beach—a much better view, I will say, than my studio apartment overlooking an alley in Venice Beach. Each morning, I would wander out from the studio my dad built for me above the garage when I was in high school to the kitchen in the main house to fix myself a cup of coffee. On the kitchen table, I would find the mound of documents and notes Uncle Henry had left of things for me to tackle while he was off teaching his law students.

Most days, I would ignore the mound, take my coffee, look out at the ocean, and mentally thank my great grandparents for choosing this gorgeous (and large by Carmel standards) spit of land to build their house. In those days, the area was considered the boondocks, based on the old picture hanging on the wall of their ground-breaking, which was surrounded by open space. While the lots had filled in since then, we still had one of the best views in town.

The sight of the happy people on the beach and the sound of the waves always helped soothe me. That and the garden that framed my view. My mom's garden. If it was warm enough, I would take my coffee out and sit on the bench in the succulent garden my mom created and ask her just what I was supposed to do with the rest of my life. The answers were about as clear as those I got from my dad when, later in the day, I would visit him in the memory care facility Uncle Henry and the very nice social worker at the geriatric psych ward had found for him before I came home.

Typically, our visits would start with him scrutinizing me like I was one of his suspects from when he was the police chief. Then, as the realization of who he was talking to would dawn, he would start with the usual question.

"Following a case?"

Our way of communicating tended to involve sharing whatever cases we were working on, whether it was me telling him about the story I was working on where the soon-to-be-ex-wife of a famous actor had died from a myste-rious fall down the stairs at their house up in the Hollywood Hills ("The husband did it," we would say in unison) or him regaling me with the tale of a billionaire who had gone missing from his oceanfront home ("The wife did it," we said for that one). For the record, we were right on both occasions.

But now, neither of us was working on a case. So, I would wait a bit after answering "no" to his question. Then he would furrow his thick gray brows and squint his eyes as another glimmer of recognition hit.

"So, you're home."

"I'm home."

"Why?"

"For you, Dad."

"I don't need your help."

"Ya kinda do, Dad."

"What will you do?"

"That's what I'm trying to figure out."

"Good luck with that."

Yeah, good luck with that. What was I going to do? I could go back to Los Angeles and come back to visit on the weekends, but the truth is, I wasn't sure that's what I wanted. I had hit a wall in Los Angeles, both personally and professionally. My on-again, off-again relationship with a manipulative asshole (I believe that's the technical term) had finally, really, for sure, ended after the sixth attempt. At least, I hoped it was over. He had an unsettling ability to draw me back in time and time again against my own best interests. Being back up in Carmel would help solidify the split as now I had those more than 300 miles between us instead of having to walk past him at the sports copy desk every day like I did at the newspaper.

That was another place I was ready to take a break from. I was a little (okay, a lot) burned out from writing 3-4 short pieces a week about the darkest underbelly of society. I had originally loved the idea of being an investigative reporter, so getting the job at the *Times* after finishing college at UCLA was a dream. Exactly what I said I wanted. But working the crime beat at a daily newspaper ultimately ended up being a lot of writing stories about people at their worst—and that can be really depressing, you know?

So, I hit a wall. As we all know, if you hit a wall often enough, it hurts, which made my return home and the open-ended hiatus from the newspaper also a chance to regroup. Not, you know, run away. Not at all. But as my dad so eloquently asked every time I visited: What was it I was actually supposed to do?

Luckily, the answer was not far off. It involved Uncle Henry's bulldog, Buster—the latest in a long line of English bulldogs and bulldog mixes I had grown up with. Carmel being a particularly dog-loving community, it was practically in the city charter that you had to have a dog. Uncle Henry loved bulldogs since his college days at Yale and was active with the local bulldog rescue group, so that's what we had.

Buster, I have to say, was a godsend. Not only a good pal to have around the house while Uncle Henry was at work, Buster also proved to be especially popular with my dad. As one of the few beings (furry or otherwise) other than Henry and me that my dad still remembered, Buster became my sidekick on the days I walked over to visit him at the center.

The routine I fell into was to walk Buster over to the assisted living center and, as I entered the lobby, let the little old ladies (and they were mostly all ladies) sitting by the door "ooh" and "aah" over him. They would bring out their silly "baby/puppy talk" voices as they reached out to pet him and told stories about their own long-gone but still beloved pets. Carmel's reputation as one of the dog-friendliest cities in the country meant they had all had at least one.

Buster was used to the attention. He ate it up, wagging his big ole brindle-colored butt back and forth in happiness as they pet him. Then, when I passed the locked door that let me into the memory care part of the center and finally reached my dad, his face would brighten at Buster's presence.

"Buster!" he would shout as I sat down and took in his appearance, which seemed to get smaller and more grizzled every time I saw him—a far cry from the large and somewhat forbidding presence he occupied during my childhood.

Then we would go through our usual patter:
"So, you're home."
"Yep. I'm home."
"Why?"
"For you, Dad."

"I don't need your help."

"Ya kinda do, Dad. Ya kinda do."

"What will you do?"

"That's what I'm trying to figure out."

"Good luck with that."

It was there I learned to pivot: "Doesn't Buster look great?"

"Buster!" His blue eyes would brighten as Buster sauntered closer, sat his big ole butt down on my dad's foot, and looked up with his slobbery face showing a contorted smile.

After a period of trial and error, I had learned that late afternoon—around 4:30—was a particularly good time to visit. The residents were starting to get ready for dinner (yes, they ate very early), which meant my dad would be seated in his spot in the dining room, and I didn't have to worry about tracking him down or waking him up from a nap. After our visit, Buster and I could then continue our walk down to the beach, take a left on Scenic Road, and head back home.

One day, I decided it might be nice to take a walk in the opposite direction and head up and into town. It was a beautiful sunny day after a dreary few weeks of constant fog and drizzle, so I thought it might be nice to extend my walk and see what was happening in good ole Carmel-by-the-Sea. I had kind of been avoiding town—and a lot of the people in town—since I got back. The nice weather and a decent visit with my dad made me think maybe it was a good time to change both patterns. I was glad I did as it was there I got the offer that would lead me into the world of luxury resorts and Hawaiian hospitality. Oh, yeah, and murder.

CHAPTER TWO

As I headed up Ocean Avenue into the bustling part of downtown Carmel-by-the-Sea, I noticed that the restaurants, shops, and galleries all looked rather quaint to me now. They were set in low-rise historic buildings—a big difference from Los Angeles, with its glee for tearing down anything historic. It was kind of fun to see what had changed since I had left and just what was passing for entertainment these days. While the exteriors of the buildings still looked the same—Carmel had one of the strictest building codes in the country (the cause of constant controversy when property changes hands)—I noted that a number of Monterey County wineries had opened tasting rooms in those buildings. What hadn't changed was the fact that as I walked by at 5:30 p.m., most everything except the restaurants had closed or was in the process of closing. This included the many many galleries—nearly 100 in a square mile and the one thing other than dogs that was a constant in the city. Although the number of galleries had only grown since the town's early days as a haven for artists, they still closed as early as 4 p.m., which is why it was unusual to see the lights still on at the Seaside Gallery.

Not only were the lights on, but as I grew closer, I could hear the sound of music, chatting, and clinking glasses. As I neared the door, I saw a small sign outside that said: Artist's Reception, 6 p.m. I looked at my watch and it was 6:10.

Tonight. Cool. Nice to see there was a little life going on in the town after all.

Buster and I crossed to the other side of the street so I could stand and watch all the happy Carmelites sipping their wine and making small talk from a safe distance. It was there I felt a presence over my left shoulder—a rather tall presence (a good 6-feet to my tall-by-most-standards 5'7" frame, based on the shadow).

"Well, well, if it isn't Samantha Powers. I've been trying to reach you since you got back into town, you know."

I turned and looked up at the immaculately coiffed vision that was Mona Reynolds, an old family friend. Now in her early 60s, Mona still looked like she stepped right out of the pages of *Vogue* magazine, where she'd been a long-time features editor. Mona had also grown up in Carmel. My mom had been her babysitter so Mona would come over to visit whenever she was in town while I was growing up. Mona idolized my mom and I idolized Mona, even if she terrified me just a bit in a benign Cruella de Ville way. I mean, there were no puppy coats, but she was always incredibly stylish and had this thick shock of black hair that over the years had morphed into a stunning silver.

"Mona! So good to see you." We hugged as I mentally compared her chic scarf, matching bag, and shoes to the Venice Beach sweatshirt and Converse tennies that had been my uniform since returning home.

Uncle Henry had mentioned that, like me, Mona recently moved back to Carmel. For her, it was six months earlier when she decided to take the job as editor-in-chief of *Carmel Today*, the local luxury lifestyle magazine. As she started tap tap tapping her foot on the sidewalk while looking at the action in the gallery across the street, I could immediately tell that Mona hadn't lost any of the manic energy of the New Yorker she had been for more than 30 years.

Then I noticed that the oh-so-chic bag that matched the scarf and shoes was moving and, upon closer inspection, contained the cutest little puppy.

"Oh my god. Did you really get a pocket puppy?"

"Oh, Sam, of course I did," said Mona. "He's not a puppy—he's three years old—and he's a Yorkie-poo. I just had to adopt him. For one, as you know, this town is crazy about dogs, and now that I'm representing *Carmel Today*, I have to fit in."

Mona gestured to Buster sitting next to me panting away. "Kind of like you are. Besides, he's adorable, don't you think? I mean, look at that little face."

And then, in what would have been unthinkable if I hadn't heard it with my own ears, Mona cooed and used the same baby/puppy voice as the ladies at my dad's assisted living center as she said, "Say hi to Sam and Buster, Cornwall, say hi to Sam…"

"Oh, Mona…"

"What?" Her voice returned to its usual timbre.

"You, too, with the puppy voice?"

"When in Carmel, Sam dear. When in Carmel," said Mona, before shifting gears (and voices). "And that's all beside the point, anyway. As I said, I have been trying to reach you. Did you get my messages?"

I had seen them. Some were still sitting "unread" on my phone and others were part of the pile of messages Uncle Henry had left sitting on the dining room table. "I did. I just haven't had time to return them."

The dark brown eyes behind the designer glasses got all squinty as Mona tried to decide how truthful I was being. "How about tomorrow, then? Have time to come over to my offices at *Carmel Today*? They're just up the street in the

Carmel Plaza building. Two floors above The Cheese Shop."

"I suppose I could do that before visiting dad."

Mona gave my shoulder a little squeeze. "I know you've been a little out of sorts since your father moved into the facility. But at least now you know he's safe. Things were looking a little dicey there for a while."

I nodded my appreciation. "I know."

"Let's set a time. I don't have any meetings in the afternoon so let me know what works. I'm serious, Sam. I have a proposition for you. One I think you might like."

Now I got the squinty eyes. "Okay... Can you at least give me a hint?"

Mona pondered a moment. "Fine. It occurred to me that a little change of pace might be good for you, and we have a travel column that could use a fresh—let's face it, younger—voice," said Mona. "Heaven knows none of the people on the staff when I took over the magazine fit that description."

"Travel column?"

"You heard me. It's a part-time position and you would really be helping me out. As I said, much of the current staff is a bit hopeless. I've been doing my best to fill holes where needed, but someone with your credentials would be a godsend."

"But I'm not a travel writer."

"I need a storyteller with a keen eye, Sam, and that's you. You're a great writer who would bring

14

a fresh and unique voice to the content. And you won't fall into the worn-out old tropes we see in the travel pieces in every other magazine."

"I don't know…"

"Again, it would only be part-time, and it would really help me out," she said. Then I got another squint through the glasses and a look up and down at my admittedly slovenly appearance. "I don't think it would be so bad for you, either. Let's talk tomorrow. How's 3 o'clock?"

Okay, I was intrigued. "That works."

Mona looked over to see someone in the gallery waving frantically at us from across the street. "And now, my dear, it appears I must make my obligatory appearance to appease my sales director." Mona waved back before whispering, "The gallery owners are big advertisers in the magazine."

Mona started to cross the street in the direction of the gallery before turning back. "Would you like to join me?"

"No. I'm not really dressed appropriately."

"That is true."

"I thought I would stop by Lizzy's place."

"Good idea. She's done a great job over there," Mona said. "Lizzy definitely picked the right town to open a new dog-friendly cafe. I take Cornwall all the time. Is she still coaching the high school tennis team?"

I nodded. "Yeah. She asked me to help out, but I haven't made it up there yet. Seems kind of silly. I haven't been on a court in years."

"You should. It would be good for you. Tomorrow, 3 p.m., Carmel Plaza. See you then."

Mona strode across the street with Cornwall struggling to adjust himself in his satchel. I could hear her say as she entered the door: "Simon, darling, this looks wonderful. What a discovery you've found in this artist."

The baby/puppy talk was long gone, and she was back to using her sophisticated *Vogue*-magazine-trained editor-in-chief voice. Nice.

"Travel column? You?"

"Yup."

"For *Carmel Today*? *Carmel Today* magazine? This *Carmel Today* magazine?"

Lizzy pulled out the latest copy of the thick glossy magazine from the rack next to the bar in her cafe, the Paws Up. She flipped to the back and opened the pages to reveal a spread with a gorgeous picture of a mountain lodge reflected in a lake and a huge headline that read "Reflections of Grandeur at Glacier National Park." At the very top of the page was the header "Splendid Adventures."

"You would be writing things like this?"

I nodded. "I think so."

"Wow. Why? I mean, why you? I mean, have you even been out of the state?"

I rolled my eyes. "I joined you in Europe for the clay court season every year on my spring break from college, Lizzy."

"I know, I know. Sorry. I exaggerate. But, still, this is a different kind of travel than you're used to."

"I agree. Mona says I would bring a unique voice."

"Ha. That is definitely true," Lizzy said, pausing and nodding to someone behind me. I looked back to see one of the patrons indicating she would like another glass of wine. "Actually, you know what, I think it's a great idea. I'm sure you would love a break from writing about murder and mayhem, especially now."

Lizzy poured a glass of rosé and gestured that she would be right back. I nodded, looking around at the cafe as I did. I hadn't really checked it out since I had been back, so it was fun to see what Lizzy had done with the place. Although only a few blocks from where Mona was attending the art gallery reception, Lizzy's cafe was far away in tone from the fancy-schmancy shops and galleries in that part of town. It wasn't the only dog-friendly establishment, though. Not by a long shot. Just the latest in a long Carmel tradition. But Lizzy had worked to bring a new angle to the concept. The Paws Up offered a more casual setting than Terry's (the legendary bar at the Cypress Inn previously owned by animal rights activist Doris Day) or the more full-service Forge in the Forest (an expansive, if touristy, restaurant and saloon that even provided a menu for dogs they called "canine cuisine").

Lizzy wanted her cafe to be a casual watering hole for locals of both the human and pet variety. While there was the occasional cat on a leash or a "support" turkey, pig, or goat, it was mostly dogs and designed as a place for the locals and their furry (or feathered) companions to go when they wanted to avoid the tourists. Of course, word on the street was that it was starting to be surprisingly popular with them as well.

Lizzy set the glass of wine down on the small table next to the customer, a thin woman with stick-straight dark red hair sitting with her stunning Irish setter, who was similarly sleek and well-coiffed. As she set it down, Lizzy covertly looked up at me and gave an almost indiscernible nod toward the woman to note the similarity in the appearances. Message received. Of course, it then made me wonder what people thought of me and Buster when we walked around town. He definitely fit Uncle Henry, with his stocky frame and love of tweed jackets, more than he did me. Or so I hoped. Truth be told, Buster's brindle coat wasn't that far off from my own auburn hair, and although I've always been on the tallish and thinnish side, my bulky sweatshirts were starting to make me look a little Buster-like. I made a mental note to start pulling something other than sweatshirts out of my closet.

Now, Lizzy looked exactly like her dog, Canoodle, who was some kind of dachshund-schnauzer-lab mix. Long and lean and incredibly athletic, with curly black hair she kept short, Lizzy also grew up in Carmel—the latest in the long line of the Icaza family on the Monterey Peninsula. Her great grandparents and my great grandparents were friends or enemies or something in between. They knew each other, let's say that. She was another somewhat recent returnee. Although she never officially moved away, Lizzy spent more than a dozen years on the professional tennis tour, where she achieved some success as a doubles specialist. When she retired and came back to town permanently, she immediately started transforming what had been a somewhat decrepit cafe space into the Paws Up. It was located in the courtyard of a building her grandmother owned that was not only off the beaten path compared to the establishments closer to Ocean Avenue but surrounded by professional offices instead of retail stores.

Lizzy and I met playing tennis together on the public courts when we were kids, but it was pretty evident early on that her skill level far surpassed mine. As sisters in everything but name—Lizzy had six brothers and I was the only child of older parents, so I hung out at their house a lot—our competitiveness was legendary. There was a point where we couldn't even rally on a tennis court without trying to annihilate each other. That was about the time I started hanging out with the kids on the school newspaper instead of the jocks, but our friendship never wavered.

"It's just, I don't know, I feel a bit of a failure," I said when Lizzy returned and started wiping down the bar for what must have been the 100th time that day.

"Failure? How can you, of all people, say that? You? Samantha Powers? The girl who was going to conquer the world?"

"And now is coming home and taking a pity job."

"Pity job? Globetrotting travel writer doesn't sound like a pity job to me."

"It kinda is."

"Do you think I'm a failure because I came home?" Lizzy asked, putting out another bowl of water for a thirsty pup.

"No, but you always meant to come home when your time on the tour was over, and you know, I didn't."

"Well, family comes first, and your dad and uncle need you," said Lizzy. "Besides, the big city hasn't been treating you all that well lately."

"Yeah, I know."

"Now, maybe if you hadn't given that big speech about never coming back—and, you know, slept with Diego after your dad's retirement party—it might have made things easier."

So, yeah, there was that. But I can explain. Diego is Lizzy's older brother. I had a crush on him growing up. A few years ago, at my dad's retirement party—which Diego attended because he worked in forensics for the county and consulted on some of my dad's cases—I was shocked to learn the attraction was mutual. Mr. Sports Copy Desk (aka the manipulative asshole) and I were on one of our many breaks, and Diego was, well, *there* looking all adorable with his shock of brown hair always falling in front of his eyes. Every time he would take his fingers to brush it back over his head, well, let's just say it was very sexy. After a few drinks and still a little raw over the death of my mom and my dad being *my dad*, I may have sidled up to Diego for a conversation, which turned into an amazing night. Then it became messy. Another mess I ran away from and part of what made coming home so challenging.

"Don't remind me," I said. "How's he doing anyway?"

"He's fine. Still at the lab in the sheriff's office in Monterey. You know, he visited your dad a lot while you were gone."

"Yeah. I know."

"When do you meet with Mona?"

"Tomorrow."

"You know, Sam, I actually think this sounds perfect. A new adventure might be just what you need," said Lizzy.

CHAPTER
THREE

Right, a new adventure. So, yeah, I took the job. My first two months at *Carmel Today* were a whirlwind of new people and new ways of doing things. On the one hand, after a decade of working at a daily newspaper, the pace of a monthly magazine was downright leisurely. On the other hand, we were not as siloed as I had been on the Metro team at the *Times*. There, I was given an assignment by my editor, researched and wrote the story, and turned it in by the deadline. Boom. Done. Move on to the next story.

Here, I was involved in—or at least could see happening around me—everything that went into producing the magazine. While one issue was in production in the art department, Mona and the other editors were looking ahead to see what stories they might want to assign to writers and photographers for issues two, three, sometimes even six months out. These included the smaller local travel pieces (new restaurants or hotels or other nearby attractions) for their newsy "Out and About" section that I would oversee along with a longer travel feature they called "Splendid Adventures."

The other big difference was that, unlike a daily newspaper where there were hundreds involved (the vast majority of whom I never met or even knew existed), it was a pretty lean team of maybe a dozen people, both in and out of the physical office, that produced the magazine. As the editor-in-chief, Mona oversaw an associate publisher, two sales reps, two staff editors, a few writers (who, like me, mainly worked either part-time or freelance), an art director, a production designer, and a couple of HR/admin types. I met them all in a whirlwind of meetings and then did my best to match the faces to the names listed in the masthead at the front of the magazine. Because I have always been terrible at names, I started using some of their weird little quirks to help me remember them. It was something that had been very helpful when covering crime scenes at the *Times*, although those tended to be a little macabre.

Here, the nicknames started with Stacy Peterson, the associate publisher, who oversaw the sales team. Since she was almost always perched atop stiletto heels, she became (in my mind only, of course) Stiletto Stacy. Ben Conners, the young production designer Mona brought on, was a nerdy little guy. He looked like people I saw at Comic-Con, where I once covered a story about an altercation between a few Klingons that turned violent, so he became "Ben Comic-Conners." Ben was working on a much-needed redesign of the magazine's website that, among other new additions, would now link to their Instagram account and provide opportunities for video and other newer media. As a new member of the editorial team and someone who would be "out and about" reporting on local events, I was asked for my input, which was a quick way to get to know everyone in the office.

As Mona had alluded to when I first talked to her outside the gallery, *Carmel Today* had gotten a bit stodgy before she took it over. This included the staff. Some of them had been with the magazine for decades—before it was acquired by a married couple that owned a number of properties, including a hotel and a winery, on the Monterey Peninsula. Part of their (and therefore Mona's) mission was to bring the magazine into the 21st century without losing the "old Carmel" flavor and rattling the local residents.

In a way, Stacy and Ben represented the two opposite forces at play. Stacy, with her stilettos and bouffant blonde hairstyle, was an old-school Carmelite who looked like she would feel right at home sipping a cocktail overlooking a golf course at a Pebble Beach country club. Ben, with his long hair and tattoos peeking out from underneath a

Marvel-inspired t-shirt, represented the young hipster Carmel Valley art crowd.

In my own way, I was also part of a duo that represented the dichotomy. The other part-time (freelance, actually) columnist was an old-timer named Terry ("Tottering Terry" to me) Cummings. Terry wrote a monthly "how I see things" type of column that verged on parody. Although Mona couldn't outright kill the column—Terry was an old family friend of the new owners—she did consign it to the interior of the real estate pages, where people would be more likely to be looking at the multimillion-dollar mansions for sale than reading about the "good ole days" when, you know, "dames were dames and you knew who they were and what to call them" and other such nonsense.

But no two people represented the two sides of the coin more than the two I ended up working with most closely: Tom Morgan, the managing editor (don't tell him but I mentally called him Toupee Tom, because, well, it was ridiculously obvious just what it was sitting on top of his dome there), and the editorial coordinator, Chelsea Plumrose, who I am somewhat ashamed to tell you I pretty much immediately started calling Fuck You Chelsea (aka FU Chelsea). I don't know what it was about her that immediately raised my hackles, but the minute she opened her mouth, I wanted to slap it right off her. Well, I do know what it was about her. It was her tone. She was very young (right out of college) and her every utterance dripped with condescension while at the same time spouting absolute nonsense.

Lest it appears that I was the only one who felt this way, I could see that was what everyone else in the office was thinking every time Chelsea opened her mouth. I would see them roll their eyes when she started in with her imperious tone (to which she was, of course, oblivious) and was just waiting for the day that someone finally called her out.

Toupee Tom was one of those who "came with the magazine" (as Mona put it). He was a stickler for doing things as they always had been done and balked at anything that might change. I have to say, though, that he was also incredibly competent at his job. Tom knew more about layouts and grammar rules and pull quotes and call outs and boxed items and all the other jargon particular to the magazine world than anyone I had ever met. In short, Tom was brilliant at what he did and a godsend to have as the magazine went through its transformation, even if he fought some of the newer ideas.

At the other extreme was FU Chelsea. Right out of J-school, she had bleached blond hair she pulled back into a perky ponytail and was almost always outfitted in black knee-high boots and a short blazer. This, she constantly informed us, was part of her "authentic personal branding," as were her social media posts, which offered tips on personal branding, and the stories on personal branding she was always pitching to Mona (and turned down on every time).

FU Chelsea was also constantly quoting her professors, one of whom she called a "personal branding guru." Another favorite was one of those who give certain grammar teachers a bad name as so many of the "rules" Chelsea so confidently espoused as gospel were, in reality, either stylistic choices or archaic or just plain wrong.

"You can't start a sentence with 'and' or 'but,'" she would tsk-tsk as she proofed a story.

"Of course, you can," Tom would say. "As long as it's not a fragment, there's nothing wrong with that."

"That's not what Strunk & White would say."

"Everything in Strunk & White is WRONG, Chelsea, wrong."

"Not according to Professor Bernstein."

Chelsea would fold her little—she was tiny, naturally—arms across her chest while Tom's face turned bright red. He would then roll his eyes so hard I thought they might come out through the back of the toupee as he tried to explain just why she was wrong, and she would pout for at least an hour afterward. Often, mid-argument, they would both turn and look to me for reassurance. As the newbie in the room and still a little raw after all that had been going on in my life, I have to admit I didn't stand up for Tom as often as I should. I would usually just nod in a nondescript way to avoid the conflict, even when those conflicts involved my stories.

It didn't help that one of her jobs was to proof-read the magazine. She would do her tsk-tsking while putting pink sticky notes lined with red pen on almost every page. Later, Tom (or Mona, if Chelsea tried going over his head) would spend an hour or so sighing and removing the majority of the notes. Every once in a while, she would catch a true typo, which she would then lord over everyone the rest of the day. Unfortunately, as much as Tom would have liked to lose Chelsea, politically he couldn't. While she wasn't one who, as Mona described, "came with the magazine" (like he did) she was the niece of the owners so had even more pull over them than ol' Tottering Terry.

Suffice it to say, the more time I spent at *Carmel Today*, the more I could see why Mona had offered me the job. The good news was, office conflicts aside, the magazine was looking better and better under Mona's leadership, which made it time to tackle the travel coverage. That was where I came in.

Mona helped ease me into the position with a few of the local "Out and About" assignments. I went with her to cover the opening of a new restaurant with a hot young chef in Pacific Grove. There, I discovered that press previews of restaurants meant crowding in with a group of other writers and eating small bites of the dishes while everyone clicked pictures on their iPhones and posted them on social media—something I duti-fully did while Mona chatted with the owners.

When the chef (who we were told had attended the Culinary Institute of America up in Napa) came out, everyone clapped and took a picture with him.

Next, I went on a "hard-hat" tour of a renovation project at the Monterey Conference Center as part of a group that included both local press and Bay Area meeting planners. We donned hard hats monogrammed with our names (sassy touch, right?) as we walked around the construction site. The center's general manager pointed out the new additions, and the planners asked questions about square footage and broadband capabilities and other things that never would have occurred to me to ask. After the official tour, a gal from the local tourism bureau took us all on a progressive tasting at some of the brewpubs that had started popping up in downtown Monterey—perhaps (it occurred to me) as a response to the slew of wine tasting rooms that had popped up in downtown Carmel.

So far, the travel writing wasn't all that bad but also not all that adventurous. I pretty much used the same skills I had at the paper—the typical reporting of what, when, where, why, and how to create as full a picture as possible of the offerings at the restaurant, the conference center, and the brewpubs. But I knew those were the easy stories—short 200-300 words and a picture and I was set. Boom.

I knew I was also going to ultimately be responsible for the longer travel feature each month and looked forward to learning how that worked. I took a look through a series of back issues and noted that the "Splendid Adventures" all looked to be around 1,000 words and ran toward the back of the magazine with the bigger feature stories. The other features typically consisted of things like an interview with whatever local celebrity they put on the cover plus an architecture or design piece or a profile of an artist or gallery or a close look at a big upcoming event like the Pebble Beach golf tournament or Concourse d'Elegance car show. The difference, of course, being that my story would focus specifically on travel.

What I hadn't yet learned was exactly what went into producing those "Splendid Adventures," in terms of picking the destination and covering it. Based on the past issues I flipped through, the stories seemed to focus on a new or renovated or some-other-reason-for-covering hotel within a larger destination. They included first-person accounts of trips as far from home as a recently expanded ecotourism lodge in New Zealand or as close as a new hotel offering discounts for those taking a car-free weekend in Santa Barbara. Based on the story she wrote in the current issue, Mona herself seemed to have taken what appeared to be an amazing trip to a new resort in the Maldives. I figured the stories would at some point involve, you know, real travel but between the website redesign and them having a backlog of stories from previous editors and writers to fill the issues, it would be a while before Mona actually assigned me one. I'll admit I was intrigued but kept my focus on my other new tasks and navigating the fascinating dynamics of the office I was inhabiting three days a week while helping Uncle Henry with the house and visiting my dad.

Finally, one day Mona called me into her office and asked me to sit down. She laid before me a printed-out email. Based on the header, it was from a Brittany Simmons at DeLuxe Travel Public Relations and titled: Invitation to Mokihana Resort & Spa Team Aloha Media Tour.

"All right, so, Sam, the Mokihana Resort on Maui has recently completed a renovation and added a new spa," Mona started.

"Hence the 'and spa' in their name."

Mona gave me her best Mona smirk (and it was a good one). "Yes, hence," she said. "Naturally, they are now interested in getting some coverage of these developments in the travel media."

"Cool."

"Which means they would like to invite some of us in the media to experience it and then write about it."

"Very cool."

"Yes, indeed. By those of us, I mean you. This will be your first feature story."

"Oh, okay, sure," I said, trying to keep my cool and not start hopping around the office singing, "I'm going to Hawaii! I'm going to Hawaii!"

Instead, I said, oh so calmly, "So, you are sending me there?"

"Not quite. They are bringing you there."

"They?"

"The resort, through their public relations firm, is inviting us—in the form of you—on a complimentary trip to experience the resort and then write about it."

"Wow. By myself?"

"No, you will be there with a group of other travel writers on a FAM." And then, before I could ask what the heck a FAM was, she said the funniest thing: "It's pretty much a Club Med without the sex."

"I'm sorry, a what?"

"That's how someone once described FAMs to me."

Again with the FAM. "I'm sorry, a what?"

"A FAM trip." Mona looked over at my confused look and sighed. "I keep forgetting you're still a newbie. Essentially, a FAM—or familiarization—trip is when a hotel or a destination has their public relations team invite a group of travel writers or meeting planners or travel agents and wholesalers to visit. They set up a jam-packed itinerary of activities to show off—familiarize, if you will—said hotel or destination so that the attendees will go back and entice people, whether it's through words via the writers or suggestions from the travel agents, to book a trip."

"Huh. Interesting," I said.

"When the trips are specifically for travel writers and not planners or agents, they're also called press or media trips," said Mona. "Basically, it's how we are able to—again—'familiarize' our-selves and our readers with new travel offerings."

Mona smiled and petted Cornwall, the Yorkie-poo, who was happily curled up in a new designer dog bed on her desk.

"And the 'Club Med without the sex' part?" I asked, trying to put the whole thing together.

"Well, while sometimes they might invite a writer on an individual trip, most often they are accomplished through group FAMs, which means you will be traveling with writers from other publications," said Mona. "The 'Club Med without the sex' is how it was first described to me and is a pretty apt description of the odd phe-nomenon of spending what can be 16-hour days being wined and dined with a group of strangers."

"Wined and dined sounds good."

"I won't lie—that part is lovely, Sam. The downside is that, as with any group endeavor…" she sighed and gave a slight nod to the crew out-side her closed door, "there is the occasional—excuse my French—asshole on the trip that can sully the experience. Truth be told, there is almost always one who is a little odd or always late or annoying in some way. Most of the time it's minor and easily ignored and can even lead to an increased sense of camaraderie among the rest of the group. There's even a joke that if you can't figure out who 'the one' is, it's you."

"I promise not to be 'the one.'"

"I know you won't, my dear. But I would be remiss if I didn't point out that it is important to remember you will be there representing the magazine. It is work and not some sort of boon-doggle. We will expect daily pictures posted on the Instagram account and website, and you will need to take extensive notes and photos and write up a 1,000-word piece when you get back."

"I know how to be a reporter, Mona."

"I know you do, Sam, but this is not inter-viewing police captains or witnesses. There's a fine line we play here. You need to be a good guest because you are there representing the magazine, but you also need to take a critical eye to the aspects of the resort and the destination that will be of interest to our readers."

"Got it. I will admit that it feels a little odd because at the paper we weren't allowed to accept any freebies—not that I was offered many cov-ering crime."

"I know. A few of the big-city papers and national travel publications are the last bastions of the separation of church and state when it comes to taking freebies. Or so they claim. The truth is even some of them take these trips or comped meals or other travel-related gifts, and have a 'don't ask, don't tell' policy among their regular contributors. Pretty much every other publication either sends writers or takes stories from freelancers who have been on one of these trips. The economics of this business just don't allow for smaller publications like ours to be able to afford to send writers to the kinds of destina-tions and hotels we need to cover for the readers."

I nodded. "Makes sense."

"The way we make it work and keep our credibility—as one of my earliest mentors once explained it to me—is that we never ask for trips or perks because then we would be beholden to them. But, if someone invites us and what they provide isn't up to par, that's on them. They are fair game. Again, when you are on-site you are a guest and should be courteous at all times, but if it ends up being an awful property or an experience that you would not recommend, then we either don't include it or maybe just bury a generic news item somewhere."

"Yup, that all makes sense."

"I don't think you are going to have a problem with this trip at all. Maui is always wonderful, and the Mokihana has a gorgeous location on the beach in Wailea. At the very least, you will be able to come back with a story about the destination. I visited the resort when it first opened years ago. It was lovely then, so with the renovations and new spa, it really should be quite nice."

"From where I sit, it sounds wonderful."

"With all the fog we've been having, a few days in Hawaii does sound grand, doesn't it?" Mona said, glancing at a new email popping up on her computer. "Unfortunately, I have to deal with the hellions that make up my staff, or I might have taken the trip myself."

"Lucky me."

"Yes. I know you will do fine, Samantha," said Mona, smiling. "That's why I hired you." The smile then faded as she took note of my outfit. While it was a huge step up from the sweatshirt and tennies I had on when she first found me standing across from the gallery with Buster, my outfit was still more aligned with a newspaper reporter's garb of comfort over style (leggings, long tunic-style sweater, and, okay, I was still wearing the tennies) than Chelsea's dress-for-success blazers or Stacy's stilettos.

"Just to be sure, why don't we go over this itinerary so I can give you an idea of the appropriate attire for each event," said Mona.

I must have looked a little concerned as she followed that up with, "Don't worry. You'll do fine. This little adventure will be good for you."

CHAPTER FOUR

H ere comes the adventure both Lizzy and Mona were so sure I needed, I thought, as the announcement was made that the plane had started its preparations for landing. I looked down from my window seat at the lush landscape, swaying palm trees, and blue ocean framing the airport in Kahului, Maui, while a tourism video began displaying similar scenes in the video monitor on my flight. It was hard not to smile at the juxtaposition of the video, the beautiful island setting below, and the bustle coming from the excited passengers around me. I wondered if any of them were my fellow travel writers as Mona's description of a "Club Med without the sex" came ringing back.

I looked around. The people surrounding me on the plane included a family of five who somehow weren't all seated together but whose matching t-shirts and constant signaling to each other were dead giveaways; a woman in a tan business suit who had closed the spreadsheets on her computer after her second Mai Tai; and what appeared to be a honeymooning couple—if the number of times they grinned at each other and then fiddled with the rings on their left hands was any indication (duh). I didn't see any of them as potential travel writers, but heck, a couple of months ago, I didn't see myself as one either.

I took a deep breath. Here it was: I was about to land in Maui and embark on my first travel-industry FAM—aka press—trip. I have to admit I preferred that moniker. As someone who'd had a verified press credential for the past ten years, it just sounded more, I don't know, official and not a boondoggle. It wasn't a boondoggle; it was work.

Not that I was complaining. As my first foray into the intricacies of the travel world, the island paradise I was floating above didn't look so bad. These four days in Hawaii were going to be just what I needed. That said, as a bit of a loner, the idea of spending up to 16 hours a day with a group of strangers (aka my fellow travel writers) did cause me a little consternation. I scanned the plane again. Really, except for the business-woman in the suit, I couldn't find anyone in my section of the plane traveling on their own. They would have to be to be joining me on the trip, right? I'm not sure what image I had of a typical travel writer, but no one around me fit.

My mind kept coming back to those two words: travel writer. It still sounded so foreign to me, and I wasn't quite sure what to expect when I landed. Most of the traveling I'd done meant throwing everything I had in a duffel and hoofing it to the closest hostel—or whatever hotel was hosting Lizzy and the other tennis players for her tournaments—when I arrived. As I scanned the plane again, I wondered how the other travelers saw me. I looked down at my outfit. I was wearing long black pants and a gray tank top under a long black cotton sweater, and, yes, tennis shoes. The outfit had passed inspection from Mona as "chic traveler," although she added a light silk scarf that I promised myself I would put back on once I got off the plane. The tennies made the cut because there were activities the itinerary indicated would require close-toed shoes. One of Mona's many helpful packing tips included the fact that you should always wear the shoes that take up the most space so hello comfortable tennies on the flight. They actually came in handy because, although most of the clothes I was bringing were designed for Maui's warm weather, the air conditioning on the plane was blasting at full speed, and it was absolutely freezing, especially down at the foot level.

I heard the final landing call, and the passengers around me continued their bustling about, as did I. Mostly, I was continually checking to make sure I still had my iPhone, my wallet, and my computer on or close to my person. Phone (left pocket), wallet (right pocket), computer (messenger bag). Phone, wallet, computer.

The final (and always reassuring) bump bump bump of the wheels on the tarmac meant we were on the ground. Following what felt like an interminable amount of time for the plane to taxi to the gate and everybody at the front of the plane to take their bags out of the overhead bins and start moving, the little slow-motion shuffle to the exit started. When they finally got to my row, I followed with the requisite tug to get the carry-on out of the overhead, and before starting my own shuffle, again did the three taps to make sure I had my laptop, phone, and wallet.

Everything safely in hand, I walked through the jetway and took in the sights and sounds of Maui's airport. The first thing I noticed was that the airport terminal wasn't enclosed, so instead of the usual air-conditioning, I had my first breath of real Hawaiian air. Ahhh. There really was something about the mix of warmth and humidity with a light breeze—the trade winds they're so often extolling—that was immediately relaxing. Even the solo-traveling businesswoman had taken off her suit jacket and had a smile on her face. I decided to do the same and added the scarf Mona had given me to bring my tank top and pants up to the business casual standards listed in the materials before continuing my walk out.

The terminal opened out to a bustling baggage claim area, where I had been told to meet Brittany Simmons, the public relations person who was overseeing the trip. Truthfully, it was hard to miss the very perky and very young—she looked right out of college (I briefly wondered if she and FU Chelsea had been sorority sisters)—woman with a sandy blond bob wearing a Chanel-style suit. Her outfit looked a little out of place in the tropical setting until you noticed the bright pink strappy stiletto sandals she was wearing with it. Mona would probably call it tropical chic, and I was glad I had added the scarf.

Brittany was standing next to a tall, tan Hawaiian-shirt-clad hunk holding a sign that said "Aloha Samantha Powers" on it. His name tag read "Elua" and then on the line below it, "Hana, Maui." A local. Nice touch.

"That's me," I said when I reached them.

"Oh, Samantha, it is so so nice to finally meet you," said Brittany, aka Blond Brittany. She pulled me into a power hug, and I could see she was probably closer to 30 than she looked at first glance. So, no go on her and Chelsea as "sisters." Her friendly tone immediately set her apart as well. Brittany then gave me a peck on the cheek and nodded to the hunk. He dutifully placed the requisite lei (plumeria, if the smell was any indication) around my neck and also gave me a kiss on the cheek. Friendly folks they have on Maui.

"Uh, thanks," I managed to utter before Brittany took over.

"And just so you know, that is the welcome we give to every guest of the Mokihana Resort & Spa, not just the VIPs and the travel media," said Brittany, who then squeaked. I swear she squeaked. "Oh, I am so glad you made it! How was your flight?"

"Not bad at all."

Her voice got very low. "I'm sorry we couldn't send you business class."

I smiled. "It really wasn't a problem."

"Oh good," she said, sighing. "Some of the others weren't too happy about it. Well, one at least."

Others? I looked around as I still hadn't spotted any travel writer candidates. "Where are they?"

"They all came in on earlier flights," Brittany said, her words increasing in speed. "You are our last pick-up. Oh, we are so glad you could come. The agency has worked with Mona Reynolds for years, of course, and we all love what she's done with *Carmel Today*. Not that it was bad before but, well, you know. Anyway, it's a beautiful magazine, and the Carmel area is such an important market for the resort. And she speaks very highly of you, of course."

"That's nice to hear," I said. "Mona told me to send you her best and that we appreciate you including me on the trip. The resort sounds wonderful."

"It really is. Now that the spa has opened, it's just perfect for the readers of *Carmel Today*. Do you have any checked bags?"

"Nope, I have everything in my carry-on."

"Fabulous. Oh, this is going to be the BEST trip. I am so excited you could join us. Just so happy…" Brittany continued babbling while simultaneously clicking messages into her iPhone and somehow balancing on the little spikes on her strappy shoes as we exited the airport into a Mokihana Resort & Spa–labeled van waiting right outside.

The over-the-top welcome continued when we reached the resort. A cold towel and some sort of tropical fruit drink were immediately thrust into my hands by a pretty young gal with long dark hair (Mimi from Hanalei) wearing a dress made out of the same Hawaiian print as the hunk. Another lei (this one made of Kukui nuts) was added to my neck. The layers around my neck were starting to look positively Elizabethan and I have to admit made me stand out a little more than I was used to or comfortable with.

As I walked up the stairs and entered the open-air lobby of the resort, I immediately noted that it had a view intended to impress. And it did. Wow. The marble entryway was filled with museum-quality sculptures and paintings, but the focal point was a view of the ocean, which was framed by gorgeous palm trees and an abundance of tropical flowers. Once I picked my jaw up off the floor, I turned to find a sea of expectant faces looking at me.

"What a gorgeous view!" I managed to croak.

"Isn't it?" Brittany was beaming. "Now let's get you settled in."

I declined the need for a bellman and—after a flurry of handshakes from more beaming staff members whose names I was never going to remember (even as I scanned their name badges in a vain attempt to try) and another power hug from Brittany—I was released with the card key to my room and instructions to be down for the opening reception at 6 o'clock. Brittany told me that the rest of the itinerary would be delivered to my room and that while everything on the itinerary was taken care of, I should bring my credit card down to the reception desk later to cover any incidentals. Before I had a chance to ask just what constituted an "incidental," she clacked off in her shoes in another direction and the greeting committee dispersed, so I headed to my room.

I glanced at my watch: 3:45 p.m. That gave me a couple of hours to decompress and answer the cacophony of voicemails and texts that had been coming in on my phone, which I planned to do the minute I hit my room.

But first, wow. Again, just wow. After a long walk down an exterior breezeway—a design element that allowed all of the rooms in the resort to face the ocean—I opened the door to my room (833) and walked down a short hall to find another spectacular view. Like the lobby, the guest rooms at the Mokihana Resort & Spa were built to capitalize on the ocean view. Mine was no exception. After throwing my things on the cart next to my bed, I walked out to the balcony and stared for a while, taking in the sight of the crystal blue waters and the sounds of the ocean crashing against the shore and local birds cavorting. *Lucky birds*, I thought.

Looking out at the beach and watching all the happy guests romping in the waves brought a smile to my face. Like the waves outside our house in Carmel, I found them to be incredibly soothing and—when added to the warm air—could feel myself relax for the first time in a long *long* time. *Part of the power of travel*, I thought, and about as far cry as you could get from my former work haunts of police departments, courthouses, county records departments, and newspaper corridors.

Work. This was work, I had to remind myself. Although I really wanted to immediately sit back on the chaise lounge that had been so conveniently placed on my balcony and take a nap, I went back into the room. It was quite well appointed. At least it looked so to me. Ridiculously large flat-screen TV? Check. Fluffy white duvet? Check. Orchid (not fake—I checked) in the bathroom alongside luxurious skin products? Check. They even had a pillow menu (in case any of the six on the bed were not to my liking) and one of those Japanese toilets with a heated seat, which I'm going to tell you right now is not something you think you need until you actually experience it. I made a note to discuss the idea of getting one at home with Uncle Henry as it would come in very handy on those cold Carmel mornings—much more than here in Hawaii. Either way, it was a very sassy touch.

Obviously, this life of luxury hotel rooms was very new to me. Based on Mona's detailed description, I knew certain things were expected, but the perfection of every detail in the room was still a pleasant surprise. After taking pictures of everything I could think of while the room was still in its pristine state, I sat on the bed. There, I noted a gorgeous watercolor print on the wall by an artist named Grant Willoughby, titled "Sunrise at Hana"; reading lights built into the bed's head-board; and a card on the bedside table from the housekeeper (Margaret, no city included) listing the next day's weather and activities. More sassy touches all around.

After a quick unpacking, I set up my computer so I could start to let everyone back in Carmel— Uncle Henry, Mona, Lizzy—know that I had arrived safely. I was posting a photo of the view from my room to the *Carmel Today* Instagram account—#MokihanaResort #MauiViews #CarmelToday—when I heard a knock at the door and a voice calling "room service."

I opened the door to find a hotel employee wearing a shirt that I had by now confirmed as the Mokihana Resort's signature print. It had the same teal blue Hawaiian pattern as the gaggle of valets and bellmen that were part of my greeting party, not to mention the Hawaiian Hunk from the airport and the lovely gal who gave me the drink and cold towel. The employee—whose name tag I noted read "Benjamin" and "Coeur d'Alene, Idaho"—was pushing a cart with a ridiculously large basket. It was filled with what at first glance appeared to be flowers, muffins, dried fruit and nuts, and bottles of freshly squeezed juice.

"I'm sorry. There must be a mistake," I said. "I didn't order this."

"No mistake," Benjamin said. "It's your welcome amenity courtesy of the general manager. This is for you as well."

Benjamin handed me a packet with my name on it while he started laying the ridiculously large basket on the table next to the ridiculously large flat-screen TV. I opened the packet and pulled out the contents. There was a folder that included a brochure for the hotel, press releases on the renovation and new spa, and bios of the resort executives. On top of it all was a series of papers labeled "Mokihana Resort & Spa Team Aloha Media Tour Itinerary for Samantha Powers." More sassy touches. They had sent a rough itinerary the week before by email (I had a printed copy in my bag just in case), but this one was filled with more details and, you know, on shiny paper and all.

The first item on the agenda was the reception Brittany mentioned, albeit using a lot more flowery language—6:00 p.m.: Team Aloha Welcome Reception on the Pool Deck. Join us on the Mokihana Resort & Spa's expansive pool deck for a wonderful island feast. Enjoy dining under the stars while watching the sun sink behind the Island of Lanai. Joining us for our launch dinner will be General Manager Philippa Chang, Director of Sales Brandon Young, and Spa Director Katrina…

My reading of the rest of the itinerary was interrupted by the ring tone of my phone. When a picture of pocket pup Cornwall appeared on the screen, I knew it was Mona. I waved to my new friend Benjamin from Coeur d'Alene, Idaho, as he let himself out and then clicked "accept."

"Aloha," I said.

"Aloha indeed," said Mona. "I saw your post. Gorgeous. How's the room? Tell me it's a suite."

"It's not a suite, but really, it's perfectly lovely."

"That may well be but, still, no suite? What's with that? Our readers don't stay in standard rooms, darling. Did they at least send an amenity?"

"It just arrived," I said.

"And?"

"It appears to be muffins and tropical juices and some beautiful flowers."

"No wine, sparkling or otherwise? Not even some Pellegrino or Fiji water?" Mona scoffed. "Whatever. Don't worry. I'm sure things will improve. What's on tap for tonight?"

I pulled out the itinerary. "A welcome reception with the general manager, the director of sales, and the spa director on the pool deck."

"Perfect. What's the dress listed as?"

"Resort casual."

"You still understand that means no shorts, right?"

"Yes. You already went over this with me. I wasn't raised by wolves, Mona."

"Much as I love them, your family was never enamored with style, Sam dear," said Mona. "Besides, as we discussed, this is your debut of sorts. You are representing the magazine. Wear the print skirt I helped you pick out last week."

"I will. Don't worry. I will make you proud."

"You always do, my dear. And now I must run as Cornwall seems to have yakked up some sort of foreign substance on my desk."

I laughed at the image of her pristine office sullied in such a manner. "Good luck."

"You, too. I can't wait to see your next posts."

I smiled and looked at the time—5:30—ouch, how did it get to be that late? Time to get ready for my "debut" as Mona called it.

CHAPTER FIVE

Time to make my debut (of sorts). Mona's words rang in my ears as at exactly 6 p.m. I smoothed the flower-print linen skirt she'd suggested I wear and tried to corral my hair back into its tie a bit more. All the humidity added to Hawaii's famous trade winds had led my auburn curls to try to make a break for it, so I pulled them back into a ponytail and added one of the plumerias from the lei as an accessory. I then took a deep breath and headed out the door. As I started heading down to the pool deck to join the rest of my travel cohorts, I dutifully adjusted the press trip name badge, which was hanging from a lanyard made from the same Hawaiian print as the hotel uniforms (yet another sassy touch).

Once I reached the pool deck, the initial vibe was less Club Med (not that I'd ever experienced one, it occurred to me) and more walking into a high school dance where you don't know a soul and are the last to arrive—even though it was only 6:04, according to my watch. I quickly scanned the crowd gathered at small high-top tables around the pool to see if I could spot anybody who looked remotely friendly. A server came by carrying a tray (Simon, Tahoe City, California). I asked him if this was indeed the press reception. I had passed by three other groups having cocktails (including a very corporate-looking one where I'd spotted the businesswoman from my flight) on my way down, so it didn't hurt to make sure. Before he could speak, I heard Brittany's unmistakable squeak and saw her waving frantically at me from the far end of the deck. I picked up one of the tropical-looking concoctions the server was carrying and made my way over.

The party was festive, I will give them that. There was a three-piece combo (ukulele, guitar, bass) on a bandstand playing Hawaiian music; a number of food stations, including a carving station with a chef at the ready; and an open bar. They were surrounded by twinkling lights and highlighted by multiple cocktail- and appetizer-bearing servers. Just beyond the bar, about a dozen people were congregating around the high-top tables. I smiled as I passed the first one, as every single person there had their camera out (mostly iPhones but also a couple of pretty high-end Nikons). They all took turns photographing the cocktails and appetizers they had arranged perfectly on the table.

Although I would have loved to join them, I continued over to Brittany—still gesturing wildly at me—at the farthest table and immediately started scanning the names of the people who stood around it. Luckily, they had created the press trip name badges so that the first names were all in large-font capital letters followed by a smaller last name on the second line and the name of the publication on the third. The second two were pretty much unreadable from a distance, but at least I could see everyone's first name.

Brittany was standing next to "ALISTAIR," a man I guessed to be at least Mona's age but not nearly as well preserved. Once I got past the orange spray tan and black dye job on both his head and goatee, I noticed the bloated and rosacea-tinted nose and cheeks indicative of someone who enjoys his libations a little too much and a round belly he attempted to hide with his sports coat. I did give him points for wearing an ascot under his polo-style shirt and sports coat. In Hawaii. An ascot.

Next to him was "TAYLOR," a tall and very skinny (I believe the expression is "heroin chic") woman who appeared to be in her late 20s. She had the pasty-white complexion of an East Coast city-dweller, with high cheekbones, dark brown eyes lined with black eyeliner, straight jet-black hair (that the humidity was not affecting), and a jet-black dress to match. Tall Taylor was standing next to "TREVOR," who could have given the Hawaiian hunk at the airport a run for his money in the looks department but in a more bland New England prep school–style way. He was the same height as Taylor, with dirty blond hair and a perpetual Derek Zoolander look on his face. If I was not mistaken, Trevor was wearing what appeared to be the Tommy Bahama separates I had seen in the window when passing the gift shop. Although their outfits could not have been more different—she dressed for a Morticia Addams look-alike contest and he for a quick game of bocce—it was pretty obvious from their body language that they were a couple.

Rounding out the table was "FRED," who totally reminded me of my Uncle Henry, down to the age (late 60s), gray hair, rumbled tweed sports jacket, black-rimmed glasses, and a constantly bemused look that—in Uncle Henry's case—enthralled his law students when it wasn't driving them crazy. Except for the fact that Fred had a well-trimmed gray beard and Henry didn't, they were mirror images of each other.

As I reached the table, Brittany and Alistair (who I, of course, immediately nicknamed "the Ascot") were deep in conversation. Well, Alistair was talking in her direction and Brittany had a pained look on her face in place of her usual perky countenance.

"...so naturally I did not give it a positive review on my radio show," Alistair said. "They've been trying to get me back in their good graces ever since."

He gave a little smirk as if to indicate his importance—self-perceived or not.

"Well, Alistair, I know you are just going to love this resort," said Brittany, trying ever so hard to bring the perky back. "They've really gone all out on the facilities. The chef is wonderful, and the new spa just sublime."

"We'll have to see, won't we?"

"You won't be disappointed."

"That's what your agency said about that wretched place in Taos, Brittany."

"Well...."

"It's okay, my dear. I know you are paid to make these places sound wonderful. What you haven't learned is that a nice bottle of Veuve Clicquot always helps the reviewing process. Then again, anything would be better than the cheap rum drinks they're trying to pawn off on us."

Brittany looked humiliated as Alistair gave her a wicked smile. "As a reminder, I'm in suite 825. The Molokini Suite," he said.

Brittany's look turned from humiliation to brief anger as the others all mouthed a surprised "suite?" at the same time.

Huh. So, this was the travel-writing industry. A far cry from the scrum of crime reporters trying to grab a lawyer for a quote during a trial. Or was it?

"Well, I just love it here," Taylor, the bone-thin gal with the jet-black hair and heavy eyeliner to match, said in strident clipped tones that belied the compliments coming from her lips. "Love it love it love it. And my photographer, Trevor here, is getting some great shots."

Everyone turned to look at her "photographer" Trevor, whose "great shot" at just that moment was an iPhone close-up of himself grinning insanely as he placed an appetizer in and out of his mouth in a boomerang-style shot.

"Uh, well, he's also an 'influencer.'"

Fred and Alistair both groaned, which made me laugh and think of Chelsea's constant "personal branding" speeches. Trevor obviously had taken the same class as she had.

"We, uh, well we loved the welcome amenity," Taylor continued, trying to save the situation. "Coconut pineapple muffins, so au courant! Reminded me of the trip I took to St. Croix for *Cosmo*."

"It would, you sycophant," Alistair the Ascot said. "I, for one, still believe in integrity..."

"Unless there's a little Veuve Clicquot involved, I'm assuming," Fred said under his breath before raising his eyebrows and giving me an Uncle Henry–like grin. I immediately loved him and hoped he wouldn't mind if I started calling him Uncle Fred.

Brittany followed Fred's gaze over to me and, realizing I was standing there, quickly pulled me into another hug—this one verging on the desperate.

"Oh, Samantha, you made it!" Brittany said. "Everybody, this is Samantha Powers with *Carmel Today*. You know, the magazine Mona Reynolds recently took over."

"Please, you can all call me Sam," I said.

"Of course. Sam, this is Alistair...." The Ascot nodded. "And Taylor and Trevor." Now forever branded in my mind as T&T. "And Fred." Fred put out his hand to shake mine and gave me another warm smile.

"Did you get all settled?" Brittany asked.

"I did. Thank you again," I said. "Everything has been wonderful."

Brittany shot Alistair a look. "It really is, isn't it?" She then looked beyond me as two people started walking onto the pool deck—corporate types based on their attire and demeanor, and the fact they appeared to give everyone and everything they passed a critical eye. "Oh, and perfect timing, there's our general manager, Philippa Chang, and our director of sales, Brandon Young."

The first person, a tall gorgeous middle-aged Asian woman wearing a perfectly tailored Hawaiian print dress paired with a strand of pearls and a dark jacket, stopped at the first table. The second—a white man of about the same height but who appeared to be about a decade younger—continued on in response to Brittany's furtive gesturing.

"That's Brandon. He just joined the resort from the Four Seasons on Oahu," Brittany whispered to me, although I noticed as he got to the table that his Mokihana Resort tag labeled him as coming from St. Louis.

"Welcome to the Mokihana Resort & Spa!" Brandon said, smiling and shaking each person's hand. When he got to me, I got a glimpse of some gorgeous baby blues paired with dark brown hair and teeth that could blind in the right light. Compared to Trevor, his looks were more corporate—complete with stylish Warby Parker–style eyeglasses and what appeared to be a bespoke sports coat (okay, so Mona's eye for fashion was starting to rub off on me a little)—but in a way that only made him better looking. Kind of a Clark Kent vibe. When he shook my hand, Brandon held it for an extra second that, combined with that dazzling smile, brought a little jolt of electricity. He was probably ten years older than I was and, being a sales dude, probably a total player, but, yowza, there was a big part of me—the part that hadn't seen any action since my last breakup from Mr. Sports Copy Desk and thought *Hawaiian fling? Why not?*—that didn't care.

Club Med WITHOUT the sex, Sam, I had to remind myself as I returned my attention to the table and noticed that, perhaps because (unlike Alistair's) Brandon's tan looked real, Alistair seemed to take an instant dislike to the man. He squinted his eyes as he sized him up and shook his hand.

"I hope Brittany is making you all feel at home," said Brandon.

Alistair gave a grunt as he continued to look him up and down like the lead lion in a pack eyeing a threat to his hierarchy.

"Very much so," said Taylor.

"As always," said Fred.

When Brandon looked back at me, I managed to blurt out. "I'm really looking forward to tomorrow's activities—spa at 10, lunch on the *King Kamehameha* at noon..." Thank god I'd read the itinerary, right?

"Oh, my dear, have you memorized the itinerary?" Alistair the Ascot said, now turning his squinty gaze in my direction. I couldn't read the tone and wondered if I should admit that I (with Mona's help) had already planned out my wardrobe for each of the events as well. As I turned to face him, he actually broke into a huge smile that changed his demeanor immensely. "I think that's charming. What a breath of fresh air."

"We have planned a wonderful series of events to show off our little pocket of paradise in addition to the offerings at the resort," said Brandon.

"I'm just happy you aren't subjecting us all to another trip on that miserable road to Hana," said Alistair. "It's just *so* not worth it unless you're going to stay out at the Hana-Maui Resort, which is, of course, quite lovely—even lovelier when they fly you there directly as I was recently."

"We realize your time is limited so are trying to showcase activities guests will enjoy while staying at *our* resort," said Brandon, smiling and handling Alistair beautifully. I was taking notes as it might help me when it came to handling the crew back at *Carmel Today*.

"I, for one, am really looking forward to the sunrise bike ride down the side of the Haleakala volcano," said Fred, raising the mood a bit. "It's something I have always wanted to do."

"It is truly spectacular," said Brandon. "But that's not for another couple of days, so in the meantime, please enjoy the food our chefs have prepared this evening. It's all taken from our restaurant menus and typical of the cuisine guests can expect here at the resort."

As we all started walking toward the food stations, I felt a little tap on my shoulder and looked back to find Alistair. "So, my dear, how is it we haven't met before?"

"I don't think we move in the same circles," I said.

"Well, of course we do. You're here, aren't you?" He smiled and again I noticed how his whole face changed as his demeanor did. His ability to change his countenance on a dime was a bit unsettling and verging on creepy.

"I have to admit I hadn't heard that Mona moved back to the West Coast and taken over *Carmel Today*. I'll have to reach out to her when I get home. I can see that she's lucky to have you. You're going to be a great asset to the magazine," he continued. Okay, so that was kind of sweet even though he didn't really know me, did he?

"Thank you."

"This isn't your very first press trip, is it?"

"Oh no. Well, first major one. I covered some local stories in the Monterey area."

"Right," he said with not a little disdain before switching gears/faces again. "Well, in case you haven't guessed, I am an old hand at these, so if there is anything I can do to help, please ask," he said. "In fact, I'm in the Molokini Suite—825—and would hate to drink my Veuve Clicquot all alone in case you would like to hear any old war stories."

Quick pass. "No, thank you," I said quickly.

Alistair put his hands up in mock surrender. "Oh, heavens. I didn't mean to be forward. Really. If there's anything I can do to help, I'm happy to do so. I've known Mona Reynolds for-ever—we were both at Conde Nast back in the '90s—and would hate for her to think I didn't help one of her proteges."

I made a mental note to ask Mona about Alistair when I got back to my room before he switched gears. "Are you looking forward to the boat ride tomorrow? It's quite the adventure, especially if you like roller coasters."

"Roller coasters?"

"The Pailolo Channel is considered one of the windiest and roughest in the Hawaiian Islands. Don't get me wrong, it's gorgeous and a must-see, but if you are at all prone to motion sickness, you'll want to make sure to use a Scopolamine patch. I'm actually surprised Brittany didn't include them in our welcome kit with a warning about the channel. When we did a similar excursion on the Ritz-Carlton's yacht last year, the marketing team did, and they are amazing. No motion sickness and no drowsiness either."

I looked around to see if Brittany was nearby to ask how to get one, but by then she was all the way across the pool deck talking to the general manager. In the meantime, I was having some pretty vivid flashbacks of uncomfortable trips on Girl Scout whale-watching excursions.

"Can I pick one up in the hotel's gift shop?"

"I'm afraid not, but as it happens, I brought an extra one if you'd like."

"That would be great. Can you bring it with you to the boat?"

"I could but you have to put it on at least four hours before the trip and, as you so astutely pointed out, we'll all be in the spa tomorrow morning. Why don't you stop by my suite to pick it up after the reception?"

I weighed a trip to his suite against the potential of spending the first day of my first press trip leaning over the side of the boat yakking up gifts like those Cornwall liked to bestow upon Mona's desk. Since (based on the room number he called out to the table) Alistair's suite was only a few doors down from mine, I decided to take him up on it. Also, this way I could tell Mona I'd seen one of the suites since, as I'd been admonished: "*Carmel Today* readers do not stay in standard rooms."

"That is very nice of you."

"Delighted to help a new generation of travel professionals," he said. "Now, my dear, why don't we see what kind of abomination they're passing off as food here…"

The rest of the reception went off without a hitch. I noticed that once all the picture-taking of the food and drinks was over (and, yes, I finally had a chance to join in so I could post some new photos), it was common among those in the travel industry—both the writers and the hotel personnel—to brag about their most recent trip or their most exotic trip or their most lurid story involving a celebrity visit to a hotel. This was especially true of Alistair the Ascot, who felt the need to top every story with one of his own. It was a lot of oneupmanship I couldn't really participate in at the moment. The new craft brewpub near the conference center in Monterey didn't really hold a lot of weight compared to a story about a particular royal's habit of sneaking hookers in through the service entrance. I did enjoy chatting with Brandon, the director of sales, he of the baby blue eyes and dazzling smile.

At one point, when it was just the two of us talking, Brandon dropped his sales persona and was actually really down-to-earth and funny. I mentioned I had been impressed by his ability to diffuse uncomfortable situations. Brandon said it was something he learned as he worked his way up in the hospitality industry. It became a game for him to be able to win over even the most difficult people. A good way to look at it, I thought.

I also asked him about St. Louis—since his tag said that was where he was from. He said that although he'd grown up there, he hadn't really been back since he left for the hospitality program at Cornell University. Right out of college, he started taking positions in luxury hotels all over the world. The way to move up in the hotel industry, he told me, was to hop from hotel to hotel. Going from a sales manager position to director of sales or from a four-star to a five-star hotel meant moving to a new property. Brandon dropped names I was familiar with (Ritz-Carlton, Four Seasons) and then some I wasn't (Langham, Rocco Forte). He had some great stories about dealing with the same kinds of characters I'd dealt with in my previous work life—murderer here, embezzler there, adulterers everywhere—without ever naming names, of course. Maybe Mona was right, and the two worlds weren't all that different.

Brandon saw Philippa, the general manager, nod in his direction and excused himself, and before I knew it, everyone was peeling off to go to their rooms. I looked around to find Alistair to ask about the seasickness patch, but he wasn't there, so I headed up to the 8th floor.

The first thing I noticed after walking past my room and around the corner to his suite, which was—as I thought—only a few doors (seven, to be exact) past mine, is that unlike my room, his had two doors. I knocked on the side with the key-hole and heard Alistair call out a greeting. I then heard the sound of footsteps get closer before he opened the door. He was wearing a Mokihana Resort & Spa bathrobe over his shirt and pants instead of the sports coat, but yes, the ascot was still properly tied.

"I'm so sorry to bother you," I said. "But you did say to come by to pick up the motion sick-ness patch."

"Yes, yes, of course," said Alistair. "No worries at all. I'm sorry I left early, but I was feeling just a little under the weather. And I can't even blame the food. I have to admit it wasn't terrible."

"I'm glad to hear that. I thought it was quite good as well."

"Come in, come in," Alistair said. He noticed my eyes widen at the immensity of his room. There was a full living room and separate dining room with a fully stocked bar that included, yes, a bottle of Veuve Clicquot resting in an ice bucket with a Mokihana Resort card beside it. "If you are wondering, I asked them to upgrade me. Never accept a standard room if you want to be taken seriously, Samantha. That's lesson number one."

Picking up the bottle, he continued, "Lesson number two is that you'll never get anything you want unless you ask."

Okay, so those were really the same lessons, weren't they? I ignored him as he popped open the bottle and poured a glass. I guess whatever was ailing him wasn't going to keep him from his Veuve Clicquot. I inwardly sighed. I really just wanted to get to my room. It had been a long day.

"Glass?"

"No, thank you. I really just want to get back to my room. It's been a long day and I still need to post some photos on our website. Can you get the patch?"

"Fine. Your loss."

Alistair headed into the bedroom with the glass, leaving the bottle on the bar. I looked around and took in the swankiness of the suite. In addition to the huge indoor living space, it had a gorgeous patio decked with multiple chaise lounges and views out to the ocean, which was now dotted with lights from the moon and stars. Sweet.

Back in the bar area, where the champagne sat, I noted the same amenity basket I had received. His had definitely been picked through as there were muffin tops missing and a few half-empty juice bottles. Then I noticed a second one right next to it that hadn't been touched at all. Did he really ask for an extra one? How tacky.

The champagne was starting to sweat water onto the bar near a leather portfolio with Alistair's named etched in gold letters on the outside. I moved the portfolio over and picked the champagne up and put it back in the bucket like the good girl that I am. (Hey, I may not have Mona's fashion sense, but my mom did raise me right).

As I moved the champagne into the bucket, I noticed a really cool lamp at the end of the bar that looked like it was carved out of Koa wood and included some really intricate designs. I picked up the lamp to get a closer look at the carvings, carefully handling it as some of the edges were really sharp. I then noticed the lights were being lowered and heard the unmistakable sound of a Jacuzzi tub being turned on in the other room. Are you kidding me? What happened to Mr. Under the Weather?

Ugh. Before I had to worry about getting a glimpse of Alistair in the altogether a la Harvey Weinstein or Charlie Rose, I decided it was a good time to skedaddle and slipped out the door.

Quite the debut, eh?

CHAPTER SIX

O kay, so here is something I learned about getting a massage (yes, it was my first): Your mind wanders all over the place (after the initial "oh my god how wonderful and amazing is THIS???" of course). I was experiencing the Mokihana Resort & Spa's signature Lomi-Lomi massage. As I learned from the materials and as dutifully recited by my therapist Bettina (Hamburg, Germany), Lomi-Lomi is a form of massage handed down by Polynesian healers called "hapuna." As now practiced in most of the resort spas in Hawaii, this means the use of long flowing strokes designed to create harmony and balance in the body.

This particular massage was something the Mokihana Resort's spa director, Katrina (yes, Bettina and Katrina—I wondered if they were related and made a mental note to check Katrina's name tag the next time I saw her to see if she was from Hamburg as well), had created specifically for the new spa. Although they were, as you may have guessed, not Hawaiian, Bettina related that Katrina and the resort's Hawaiian cultural advisor had consulted with local hapuna so they could base the treatments on traditional Lomi-Lomi techniques. I listened dutifully for as long as possible, but after a while, it started to sound like "la la la la la la" or, perhaps more accurately, "lomi lomi lomi lomi."

But, again, here's the thing: While you're lying there with your face looking down on the floor—where they had placed a plumeria flower (nice touch, right?!)—having your back muscles pummeled out (a wonderful feeling if there ever was one), you can't DO anything else. If you're like me, your mind starts to wander. At first, I started to think about how I would describe the experience in my story for the magazine...

Chief among the attributes of the renovated Mokihana Resort is the new spa, which takes advantage of its seaside location by placing the treatment rooms in thatched huts located above a secluded cove. The sound of the waves hitting the shore blends with the light breezes and the aromatherapy oils to create an experience that....

That's about as far as I got before my mind really let go and images and voices started blending. There was Mona and pocket pup Cornwall peeking out from his matching bag on the sidewalk across from the gallery as she offered me the travel writing position. Uncle Henry telling me that he thought it would be best for all of us if I were to continue to stay with him and Buster while we took care of my dad. Lizzy dealing with the dozens of dogs of all sizes that were at the Paws Up each afternoon for their Yappy Hour. It was at that point that Lizzy's brother Diego flashed by as well. The image was of his shy smile and that flop of dark brown hair shading his warm brown eyes as he nodded from across the gaggle of dogs at Lizzy's when I first got back to town. That segued to memories of the night we snuck away from my dad's retirement party and the momentary balm it provided at the time.

The warm feeling conjured by Diego's sweet grin soon transformed into Brandon's glistening smile from the night before and then, without warning, to Alistair's leering gaze. I could feel my body do a little jolt in horror. God, that was awful.

Club Med WITHOUT the sex, Mona had promised. I laughed to myself (at least I hoped it was to myself) and realized I still needed to tell her all that had happened. I had managed to post some pictures of the opening reception on the Instagram page and give the event a quick write-up for the website, but that was about it before crashing the night before.

Bettina really sank her knuckles into one of the big ole knots I always had going in my upper back. I could feel my body relax even further and the images start to recede. Then, suddenly, out of my foggy reverie, I started to hear the sound of steps and people's voices, and what sounded like "amantha ower." I looked up to see what was going on.

"Bleisuthei oeithe," I said. Or something to that effect.

"Let me see what's going on," Bettina said, helpfully. She stepped out of the massage hut and closed the curtains for privacy. I heard hushed voices and sat up, pulling the sheets up to cover myself on the table. Bettina soon returned and said they wanted to talk to me and that she would step out so that I could put on a robe and join the security people outside.

Security people? What the?? I put on my robe—not a personal robe, of course, but the lovely robe the Mokihana Resort & Spa had provided me (so soft!)—and headed out to find out what was going on.

I soon found myself sitting around a table in the spa's courtyard with about a half dozen other people. We were all similarly dressed in Mokihana Resort & Spa robes and wearing the telltale sheet marks on our faces from the massage table. I recognized Fred, Taylor, and Trevor from our table at the reception the night before. We each gave each other a little nod of recognition and shrug of confusion as to what the heck was going on. I was just noticing that the one person who was missing from our table was creepy Alistair the Ascot when a very serious-looking group that included a man I didn't recognize—tall, handsome, and definitely a police detective, if the gun on his hip and the badge clipped to his well pressed Hawaiian shirt were any indication (rhetorical: they were)—arrived.

Philippa Chang, the elegant-looking woman Brittany had pointed out as the general manager of the resort (and whose name tag I could now see identified her as being from Honolulu), nodded to the detective and then began speaking.

"I am so sorry to have to tell you all this…" Philippa started. "But this morning we found Alistair Sinclair in his room, and well, he's dead."

People gasped—they literally gasped. I always thought that was kind of an overblown thing they did in movies, but nope, enough people sucked in air together that it was audible. I don't think I was one of them, but I do remember feeling pretty shocked to learn that someone who'd been alive—creepy, but alive—not 12 hours before was dead.

Then my instincts kicked in—from my dad and my years on the crime beat—and I started looking around the room to see everybody's reactions. Brittany, who was standing behind Philippa Chang, was biting her nails frantically as her face drained of all color. Brandon, the sales dude, put an arm around her shoulder in an attempt to console her with not a hint of his glistening teeth to be found. Next to them, Philippa, the general manager—who had a new (and, I might add, also quite stunning) Hawaiian-print dress under her business jacket—was the image of calm. She stood perfectly still and poised while allowing everyone to take in the news.

I scanned the circle of robe-clad writers. Taylor was glaring at Trevor, who was taking a picture of himself frowning with his phone. Fred was watching both of them with a bemused look before continuing his own tour of the table. When we got to each other, we met eyes, gave each other a silent eyebrow raise-nod combination, then continued to look around.

There were three writers I hadn't met the night before: a tiny white woman who appeared to be at least 80 and probably weighed about the same in pounds sucking down the smoothie the lovely Mokihana Resort & Spa staff had placed before us; a middle-aged follicly challenged Black man whose large upper body suggested he had been either a football player or a bodybuilder in his youth trying his best to make sure his spa robe completely covered him (almost but not quite); and a manic young (maybe 20-something) kid with pink skin and spiky red hair who seemed to find it difficult to sit still in his chair.

Once Philippa Chang made sure the news had sunk in, she continued. "We don't really know yet what happened," said Philippa. "When Alistair didn't show up for his spa appointment, we asked housekeeping to check his room, and … well, they found him lying on the floor. Out of an abundance of caution, we called both an ambulance and the Maui Police Department. To that end, I'd like to introduce Detective Roger Kai. Detective Kai."

"Thank you," said Detective Kai. "As Ms. Chang just said, Alistair Sinclair was found dead in his room. We were called in to take a look once the EMTs called the time of death. After a preliminary walk through the room with the medical examiner, the circumstances are such that we believe his death warrants more investigation."

His death warrants more investigation? Now that was interesting. I scanned the room again—again stopping and meeting eyes with Fred for a bigger eyebrow raise before moving on to gaze upon the others' looks of consternation and confusion.

"What we would like to do now," Detective Kai said, "is to meet with each of you separately."

Kai consulted his notes. "And we'd like to start with Samantha Powers."

Huh? I could feel all the eyes turning to look at me. "Why me?" I asked.

"According to the security footage in the hallway outside of Alistair's suite, you were the last person to see him alive," said Kai.

Oh, yeah, I suppose there was that.

A short time later, I found myself in the spa's relaxation room—a lovely room that smelled like lavender and eucalyptus and had soothing music and plush couches that I would definitely be calling out in the story as quite exquisite—talking to Detective Kai. He had set up two chairs on either side of a table I'm guessing they usually used for manicures. Kai gestured toward the one opposite him. He sat down in the chair next to a file folder and a legal pad and pulled out a pen.

"Thank you for letting me get dressed," I said as I sat down. I did feel much better to be in my own clothes and not wearing the spa robe, which—incredibly soft as it may be—lent an air of vulnerability to the proceedings.

"You're welcome," Kai said, smiling. It was a good one, too. Detective Kai looked to be about my age—mid-30s—and kept his black hair clipped short. Between the short hair, ramrod straight posture, aviator-style sunglasses, and perfectly ironed shirt with the meticulously placed badge, Kai gave the impression of a background in the military, but his dark brown eyes had a warm intelligence to them.

"I'm sorry for your loss," he said.

"Loss? You mean Alistair?" I asked. "I just met him last night."

"And yet you entered his room."

"Suite."

"Suite?"

"Yes, he had a suite. None of the rest of us have suites, but he made a point of telling us that he requested an upgrade at the opening reception."

Kai smiled a little as he nodded and jotted that down. "Okay, so you entered his suite because…"

"I entered his suite because he told me he had a seasickness patch for the boat ride we were supposed to take today—oh, man, I guess that's off now, huh?"

"Most likely," Kai said as he jotted some more notes on the legal pad.

"Anyway, Alistair said he had a patch that would keep me from getting seasick and that I should pick it up from his room—sorry, suite—after the reception," I said.

"Do you have the patch on you now?"

"No. I got there, and he pulled a—well, you know the Harvey Weinstein story, right?" Kai nodded. "Well, he told me he was getting the patch and left the living room area, but then I noticed the lights dim so I skedaddled. Nothing happened."

"Nothing except he died," he said in a non-committal sort of way as he continued to jot notes onto the legal pad. I have to admit it was a nice move as his neutral tone and movements allowed him to gauge my reaction. He followed that with an uncomfortable moment of silence that, had I been hiding something, might just lead me to say something to implicate myself. All things I'd learned from my dad. Kudos, Detective Kai. That's some darn good police work.

As Detective Kai continued writing on his pad, I noticed that he had inadvertently nudged the folder that was tucked beneath it. I could now see just a bit of the writing inside—something something -uma?— on what appeared to be the chrono, which is the chronological log of the scene from the moment the officers entered.

"So…" I finally said, the curiosity getting the best of me. "What happened? Do you have a cause of death? Did he drown in the Jacuzzi tub? I could hear him start that thing up—another reason for the quick skedaddling on my part."

Kai again gave the teeniest of smiles before continuing. "I'm not at liberty to discuss the particulars."

"I understand. I used to cover crime for the *Times* so this is not all that unfamiliar to me—I've just never been on this side of the table, as it were."

"You also have family involved in law enforcement, if I'm not mistaken."

"You checked up on me?"

"Kinda part of my job."

"Yes, my dad was the Carmel police chief," I said. "He's in a memory care center now with Alzheimer's."

"I'm so sorry."

"I appreciate that. It's been difficult to watch it happen to such an intelligent man."

Detective Kai looked me in straight in the eyes, and I got a sympathetic smile. It was a nice one and, like his eyes, quite warm, and I noticed— without even meaning to, really—that he wasn't wearing a wedding ring. I also noticed he was wearing a few thin braided leather bracelets of the type I'd usually seen on surfers, an interesting juxtaposition with the pressed military bearing that made up the rest of his image.

"Well, Ms. Powers," he said, turning back to his pad. "Obviously, we are just in the preliminary stages of our investigation into Mr. Sinclair's death, so we're going to have to ask everyone involved with this trip not to leave the island — or even, until we say otherwise, this hotel — until we have a better understanding of just what happened."

As he moved the legal pad back away from the file folder, the sheet inside moved a bit more and I could see "...nial trauma" written on the paper. Yes, it was upside down, but my skill at picking out important words upside down was finely honed during my years on the crime beat. Truthfully, it was something else my dad taught me as a youngster that came in super handy all the way through school. The only thing I could think of that might include those words — or part of words — was cranial trauma. In other words, Alistair hit his head on something. Interesting, but it really could mean anything when it came to the cause of death.

"So, what, you are placing us all under a sort of house arrest?" I asked, pretending I didn't see it.

"That's not legally accurate at all."

"But we are being confined to this place."

"If it makes you happy to see it that way, Ms. Powers, sure. Really, we just need all of you who knew the deceased to stay put until we learn more about what happened. Seems to me that you, of all people, should understand that."

"I do. It's just funny being told I have to stay put in a world-class luxury resort and spa. I mean, I suppose there could be worse places for that to happen."

Okay, so I was getting a little snarky. Humor was my defense mechanism to uncomfortable situations, and come on, this was all getting a little uncomfortable, right?

"As I said, just don't leave the grounds until we tell you it's okay." No smile this time.

"Sorry. It's just all a little overwhelming. I mean, this is my first trip as a travel writer, and I thought I'd be writing about thread counts and roller coaster boat rides, and instead I got this."

"Hopefully, we can straighten this all out soon, and you'll still get to do your job." I got the smile again. Man, I liked his smile.

"Thanks." I smiled back. It seemed weird because, you know, a man was dead and all, but it was all kind of funny, right? I mean, here I was being told by a handsome detective that we were being confined to our sumptuous lodgings with gorgeous views of the ocean during a suspicious death investigation.

I wondered if that should be the lead to my story. You know, something like: *Of all the places to be confined during the investigation of a suspicious death, the luxurious Mokihana Resort & Spa really can't be topped...*

CHAPTER SEVEN

"That should not be the lead to your story," said Mona when I returned to my room and called and gave her the news. I sat on the bed, which had already been made up and included a new card from the housekeeper (still Margaret, no city included) that listed the day's weather (83 degrees) and complimentary activities (lei making by the pool at 2! hula lessons at 4:30!).

"It was a joke," I assured her.

"It's not funny. Not funny at all. Nothing about this is funny. A, Alistair Sinclair is dead. May he rest in peace, although there won't be much peace if I know anything about him, and I do..."

"He mentioned you were both at Conde Nast back in the 1990s."

"Pffft. That would be a stretch. I was an associate features editor at *Vogue*, and he was a little freelance puffer who would ride the elevators pitching any ear he could catch. Sometimes he would get a pity front-of-book assignment from the newbies at *Conde Nast Traveler*, but the rest of us became quite adept at spotting him and darting into the ladies room."

"Obviously, he became at least somewhat successful..."

"You mean that little public radio show of his? I suppose that helped him achieve what he wanted—invitations to all the best hotels—but beyond that he is, was, still a little puffer pitching anyone who would listen. He just did it using email blasts instead of riding up and down the 6th Avenue elevators."

"Got it. And B?"

"B?"

"You said A, Alistair is dead..."

"Oh, yes, and B, one of my writers is embroiled in this nastiness. What do they plan to do with you all now?"

"Well, the boat ride was cancelled, obviously."

"Obviously."

"At the moment, we are all resort bound, but I got a text from Brittany saying that they would still hold the scheduled luau this evening since it's here on the property."

"I hope they clear this up soon," said Mona. "The pictures you are posting of the resort are great, but I need you to explore more than the resort, my dear. Everyone's written about the Haleakala bike ride, but *Town & Country* just featured a new path through a eucalyptus grove that can be accessed on the way down. I'd love for you to find a similarly unique twist on an island adventure for our readers."

"I'll do my best."

"I'm sure you will, Sam. Sorry again for not warning you about dearly departed Alistair. I should have looked more closely at the attendee list."

"So... this is all kind of crazy, huh?" I asked Fred a few hours later at the luau. We all sat at a long table facing the beach under a gorgeous full moon. I could hear the ocean waves lapping nearby, and as with everything else, the hotel had gone all out on the decor and drinks and food and music. Because of the circumstances, though, the atmosphere was not exactly the "fun and festive group luau" they had promoted on the itinerary.

They did try, though. They really did, and before Fred could answer me, a gaggle of hula dancers—both male and female—took the stage. They were followed by a middle-aged man with a broad deeply tanned face, salt-and-pepper hair, and an infectious smile. He was wearing a really cool bone necklace in the shape of a fishhook under his Mokihana staff Hawaiian shirt. He introduced himself as Clive Kealoha, the resort's Hawaiian cultural advisor. Clive then presented each of the dancers, told us about the awards the troupe had recently won at the annual Merrie Monarch festival in Hilo, and talked us through the cultural elements of the movements we were about to see. Prodded by Brittany, he also mentioned that he meets regularly with each department at the resort in an effort to weave more authentic Hawaiian customs and protocols into their offerings.

Clive finished by saying that he would be available at any time to answer questions or provide more information for our stories. He then signaled to the band and the dancers that they could begin. I tapped the information he gave us down in the notes app on my phone and made a mental note to follow up later for some quotes. Then, after taking a few pictures, I sat back and got lost in the beautiful movements of the dancers.

When the hula dancers finished their numbers, we all applauded, and a soft ukulele started playing in the background as they began bringing the first of our many courses to the table. I was seated between Fred and Taylor, who I noted seemed to have had enough of Trevor and also had quite a bit to drink. Taylor had her back turned to him, and when she saw him take another one of his ridiculous selfies, she took another swig from her drink. Maybe this was her own personal drinking game. That did not bode well for the evening. The selfie Trevor was taking this time was with Brittany. She was seated to his right and had her head in her phone clicking away with a dour expression on her face until the iPhone camera came out and her expression immediately changed from dour to perky.

I turned back to Fred. "So, again, the whole Alistair thing is crazy, am I right?"

"Yep, pretty crazy."

"Craziest thing you've ever had happen on a press trip?"

"I've been on a lot of press trips."

"With this kind of mystery?"

"Yes, Nancy Drew. Mysteries galore. Although, okay, this is the first death, and it is pretty crazy." Fred gave me an Uncle Henry–style bemused smile and took a bite of the tuna sashimi topped with a basil reduction and wasabi foam that had been set before us. He closed his eyes and gave a little moan of happiness.

"This," he said, gesturing to the decadent food and the over-the-top party that had been put on just for the seven of us, "will keep you in this business."

I smiled. I could see how this kind of treatment could get a little addictive. I turned away from a blissed-out Fred and looked back at Taylor, who was not enjoying the festivities nearly as much as Fred. Or, really, at all.

"You seem kind of sad," I said to her. "Had you known Alistair long?"

"Of course, I knew the asshole," said Taylor, who I noted was still wearing black and probably not out of any mourning for Alistair. "We are—were—both based in New York, so I had to endure him at all of the travel-industry events in the city. He always held court as if he was fucking royalty. When I first started out, I was freelancing. We were constantly pitching the same magazines, so he was always trying to smear my name. He even told one of my editors that I faked some quotes from my trip to Aruba. Those quotes were all fact checked…" Her eyes narrowed a little as she looked at my name tag to remember who she was talking to.

"Sam," I offered helpfully.

"Those quotes were fact checked with the source, Sam. Fact checked."

"That must have been frustrating."

"Pffft." Taylor took another swig from her cocktail and closed her eyes as she did a slow collapse back into her chair. I thought she was down for the count, but then she suddenly sat back up and continued. "Then, when I became a staffer at *Cosmo*, his tune changed. Like 180 degrees changed. Acted like we were the best buds in the world and was constantly pitching me story ideas—like, oh sure, we're going to send HIM to, well, ANYWHERE, representing *COSMO*. Ha!" Taylor's huge guffaw surprised me—and I think herself—as she then looked at me as if she couldn't remember why she was speaking to me.

"Who are you again?"

I pointed to the name tag on my lanyard. "Sam. *Carmel Today* magazine."

"Right." She took another swig and repeated the slow collapse back into her chair and closed her eyes again.

I turned back to Fred and met his raised eyebrows at her antics with my own.

"So, that was interesting," I said.

"Indeed," said Fred.

"What's your take?"

"I happen to think it was Professor Plum in the study with the candlestick. You?"

"Come on."

"I get it. It must feel weird since you were the last person to enter his room."

"How do you know that?"

"That's what they told us at the spa, remember?"

"Oh, yeah. I guess that's accurate. Technically, we still don't even know the cause of death, do we?" I said. (As I mentioned, a preliminary report of cranial trauma could mean a lot of things—including simply falling out of a Jacuzzi tub—but I didn't want Fred to know that I knew about that.) "Do you think it was anything other than natural causes?"

"With what his arteries must look like, it's hard to believe it wasn't natural," Fred said. "Although, let's face it, there were a lot of people—including some at this very table, as you have discovered—who would have loved to see Alistair Sinclair dead. The stories about him are epic. I should know as I've been on this circuit long enough to see some of them go down."

"Do tell."

"You do know he built his house with items from the hotels and resorts he visited, right? I don't mean towels and robes and miniature bottles of shampoo. He would request shower heads, wall sconces, artwork, even bed frames after a visit, and promise positive coverage on his radio show. Didn't make him particularly popular with the hotel folks—unless, of course, he gave them a rave review, and then they loved him. Those that didn't accede to his request he did his best to blackball with poor reviews."

"That makes him a cad but…"

"Okay, let's try this. You point in any direction, and I'll tell you what Alistair did to the poor schmo at the other end of your finger."

I started with the tiny older woman to Fred's left who had been sucking down the smoothie earlier at the spa.

"Ah, Dorothy. Sweet woman. Used to write for all the in-flight magazines, among others. These days her only regular assignments are for her retirement community's newsletter and a little blog she started. Alistair saw to that by finagling assignments from her editors when she took some time off while her husband was dying."

"Oh god, that's awful."

"Despicable. Dorothy still wrangles her way onto a junket like this one now and then based on her past outlets and a long-lapsed membership in the Society of American Travel Writers, but since Alistair knows she's a bit of a phony, she has to give him what he wants."

"Ewww."

"Oh, no, not that. Old Alistair likes—liked— them young. More like you." He took a beat. "What were you doing in his suite anyway?"

"He told me he had a Scopolamine patch that would help ease any motion sickness on the boat ride."

Fred gave me another Uncle Henry–like look over his glasses, then shrugged and continued. "With Dorothy, he made her send all of her amenities and gifts from the hotels to his room. Poor old dear hasn't tasted a free muffin or worn a free cap in years."

So, that's why he had two baskets in his room.

"And it's not even like he needed—or even really wanted—the stuff," Fred continued. "He usually gave it to his interns—unpaid interns, mind you—when he got home. He just liked having something over her."

"Creepy as hell but still not a reason to murder someone."

"You didn't know Alistair. The man could try the patience of a saint. Once, on a trip to Tibet, a Buddhist monk punched him in the face."

Okay, so that was pretty funny. I looked to my right and saw the large man who'd had trouble fitting into his spa robe on the other side of Trevor and Brittany. He was talking to Brandon, the director of sales. "Okay, who's that?"

"Ah, Brian. He's an editor with a meetings-industry magazine. It goes out to corporate meeting planners, upscale ones at that. Nice publication, part of a big conglomerate. And, yes, he once had a tussle with Alistair. Years ago, on a train ride through the Canadian Rockies, Alistair stole his window seat during the most scenic part of the trip."

"Petty."

"Petty is Alistair's middle name—to the point that the savvy PR firms usually send him on an individual FAM versus a group press trip like this one. His behavior tends to sully the experience for the other writers. They must have been desperate—or incredibly naïve," he nodded in Brittany's direction, "to include him on this one."

"You really do know this industry," I said. "So, the only writer I don't know yet is that guy." I pointed to the manic 20-something with the pink face and spiky red hair seated on the other side of Dorothy next to a young hotel employee—easy to spot as he was wearing the Mokihana staff Hawaiian shirt and a name tag (one I couldn't read from this distance)—that I hadn't met yet. They both had the kind of young eager faces and wiry bodies that indicated they hadn't been out of college very long and were chatting away like kindred spirits.

"Mac. Nice kid. He started writing and attending trips a few years ago for *Adventure Man* magazine, which was founded by his uncle probably 40 years ago. Like a lot of magazines, it's not what it was—more of a digital publication these days," said Fred with a sigh. "But it does have still have a readership."

"Who do you write for, Fred?"

"The *Tribune*. Well, their syndicate—you know, the stuff they send to all the small papers still eking out an existence through repurposing material. Hard for an old saw like me to leave the newspaper game, but I can tell you it isn't what it once was."

"Hey, I worked for the *Times*. I hear you."

"You did? You work with Bill Patton?"

"Not in the travel section. I covered crime. You know, murder, mayhem."

"So, this is right up your alley."

"I suppose. I mean, again, we still don't know how Alistair died, do we?"

"True. As I said, with the way he lived—all the rich food and alcohol he consumed on a daily basis—I doubt Alistair was the paragon of health, although maybe we should ask Brittany about that," Fred said with a gleam in his eye.

I leaned back behind the chairs—bypassing the passed-out Taylor and Trevor, who was busy choosing filters for the selfie he took with Brittany—to talk to Brittany.

"So, Brittany, did you know Alistair well?"

Brittany leaned back to answer me. "Only professionally through my colleagues at the agency. I mean, the man had his quirks, but everyone loved him," she said a little too quickly and not particularly convincingly.

I smiled at her continued sublimating of her true feelings, then noticed Brandon take a call and nod to Brittany. She excused herself to join him and Clive and the young employee I hadn't met yet off to the side of the table. From what I could see, there was a lot of nodding and chatting and nodding. Then they walked back over to the table and found a lot of expectant faces waiting, mine included.

Brandon smiled that million-watt smile of his as he addressed the table, at one point meeting my eyes and giving a slight nod that made my knees buckle a bit—or they would have if I hadn't been sitting down. Damn hormones.

"I'm sure you are all wondering what's going on at this point," Brandon said. "I just heard from Ms. Chang, our general manager. She talked to Detective Kai. He said they are still waiting for the autopsy results and indicated it could be another day or two before they know exactly what happened. The good news is they decided that because you are all here as a Mokihana-sponsored group, you don't have to be confined solely to the resort anymore."

"Thank god," said Fred quietly to me and gesturing at the gorgeous scene before us. "I mean, how would we survive in such surroundings?"

"What we would like to do is continue with the original press trip itinerary," Brandon continued.

I looked to see how people were reacting to the news, and the faces all seemed quite happy—if a little sloshed (aided by the constant filling of our wine glasses by the ever-present staff). No one seemed to be mourning ole Alistair.

"We so appreciate all of your patience and understanding about this and naturally hope it doesn't affect your experience of the Mokihana Resort & Spa," Brittany continued for Brandon, in her chipperest possible voice before pulling out the itinerary. "As you know, tomorrow you all are scheduled to have breakfast at leisure—just sign everything to your room—and then at 8 a.m. we will convene in the lobby as scheduled for our trip to the Upcountry farms and ranches. One housekeeping note: Since horseback riding is first on the agenda, make sure to wear your long pants and close-toed shoes. If you want to change clothes before we continue on to the rest of the tour, feel free to bring a small bag as there will be an opportunity to change and a place to leave your belongings on the van."

Horseback riding. Ugh. I knew it was on the agenda but had been trying to ignore that fact as I had never had great experiences around the beasts.

Brittany gestured to the young employee we hadn't met yet. "Also, if you haven't met him yet, Frank here works on our activity staff and oversees the kid's club. He can tell you all about those offerings tomorrow when he serves as our guide for our Upcountry tour. This includes the horseback ride at Kapena Ranch, a trip to Maui's famous lavender and goat cheese farms, and of course, the winery up in Ulupalakua."

That one got a lot of smiles and murmurs. Frank—who still had the goofy energy of a kid himself along with a Charlie Brown face to match—waved to us all as a way of introducing himself.

We dutifully waved back. The energy seemed to jolt Taylor out of her stupor. She unsteadily stood up and lifted her glass in a toast.

"To Alistair," said Taylor, while everyone tentatively raised their glasses and looked at each other warily. "I'm sure he's asking for a bigger suite and a fresh bucket of ice in hell."

CHAPTER EIGHT

I was still full from the dinner the night before, so instead of going down to the dining room for a big breakfast, I grabbed a coffee and a smoothie from the lovely gal (Simone, Harrisburg, Pennsylvania) at the cart in the lobby. I then spent what little time I had before our early morning start sorting through my photographs to decide which to post and what to say about our inter-esting—to say the least—luau experience. I picked photos of the hula dancers, the table setting, a couple of dishes, the singer playing the ukulele, and some tropical cocktails. I then posted them to the *Carmel Today* sites and looked through the other photographs I had taken on the trip.

Maybe ole Alistair did just slip getting out of the Jacuzzi or drop dead of a heart attack and hit his head on the way down. In the event he did not it didn't hurt to look at the people assembled at the luau to see if any looked like the type of person who might bonk a person on the head. As Fred said, almost everyone had a potential reason to dislike him (even if I didn't know them all) but enough to assault or possibly murder him?

I scanned the images of everyone involved with the trip. They included Brittany, Brandon, Frank, Clive, and Philippa Chang on the hotel side and, from the travel writer group, Fred, Taylor, Trevor, Dorothy, Brian, and Mac. From what I could see from the luau photos, no one at the table had a care in the world—if you discounted Taylor's drunken rant and Brittany's continually furrowed brow at her press trip going so seriously awry as she click click clicked into her phone to keep rescheduling our plans. Really, it was hard to see that any of them could have had anything to do with Alistair's death, but as I was about to spend the day with them, perhaps I would learn more.

Right at 8 a.m., I met the others at the porte-co-chere (for the uninitiated, of which I have to admit I was one, it's the overhang outside the lobby where the cars drive up) in my horseback riding garb: jeans, tank top, light wind breaker, tennies, and the lovely Mokihana Resort cap that had been left in my room the night before. A long black van with the Mokihana Resort & Spa logo emblazoned across the side was waiting for us outside alongside Brittany, Brandon, Frank, and a tall, thin dark-skinned man in a chef's toque and white jacket that said "Executive Chef Marc Wambaa." The name was sewn into his chef's garb, so he didn't have the usual name tag that might have told me where he was from, which (in case you haven't guessed by now) had become somewhat of a game for me and a way to remember their names, even if I did have the tags to help me.

Fred was already there, as were Brian, from the meetings magazine (wearing khakis and a Northwestern University t-shirt); too-cool-for-school Taylor (who'd upgraded from her usual black to a dark gray ensemble that looked right out of the Patagonia catalog); and Mac, the *Adventure Man* kid, who was appropriately dressed in some really top-notch adventure-man-style gear. Prompt group. I was glad I wasn't the last one to arrive. Soon, Trevor came skipping out waving a hat I'm assuming he had left behind followed by tiny Dorothy, still munching on a muffin as she skedaddled across the lobby to join us. Hard to see where she was putting all the food we were eating on that 80-pound frame, but I have to say she looked truly exuberant for the first time on the trip.

"We are so excited to be able to continue with today's scheduled itinerary," said Brittany once we were all assembled. She was dressed a little more casually today, although her riding pants and stylish boots were perfectly on point for our first stop at the ranch. Her hair was still flawlessly coiffed, and it made me wonder how long that blow-out took every day, especially in the Hawaiian humidity.

"Today, after our horseback ride at Kapena Ranch," said Brittany, "we will be seeing a few of the wonderful local farms that are not only popular activities for visitors to Maui, but also provide many of the products that Chef Marc uses in the menus he creates for the resort."

The man in the chef's outfit waved, and in what sounded like an accent from one of the Caribbean islands, told us that if we had any questions, he would be happy to meet with us after our tours. Another person I made a note to follow up with for some quotes while letting the others start trooping into the van. As I waited for my turn, out of the corner of my eye, I saw the unmistakable military posture and clipped strides of Detective Kai as he made his way behind us into the lobby. He turned as I turned, and I caught his eye—or at least the reflection of his aviator-style sunglasses—as he passed. He gave a small nod and a glimpse of a smile indicating that he'd seen me, but then disappeared behind a pillar. Interesting.

Before I could linger any longer to see who he might be meeting, it was my turn to board. Soon we were driving out of the area of luxury resorts and manicured beaches found on Maui's southern shores. We made our way north through the middle of the island, the narrowest area from south to north, and drove past a defunct sugar cane refinery before heading up into the hills below Haleakala, the volcano we would be riding our bikes down the next morning. The earth was lush and rust-colored and surrounded by green fields. The sky offered up the occasional rainbow that followed sporadic rain showers hitting the windshield as we started up a small rural road surrounded by thick groves of various crops.

As we made our way, Frank—who, again, had such a cherubic little Charlie Brown–like face that I had to refrain from reaching out and squeezing his cheek every time he spoke, and whose name tag (which I could now read) had him from Tempe, Arizona—stood at the front and used the provided microphone to give us a bit of the history of the island. Frank prefaced his remarks by saying the information he would be giving us had been created in consultation with the resort's cultural expert, Clive Kealoha, who we had met the night before and came from one of the oldest families on the island. The materials were the same ones all of the resort guides would be providing on tours and at the kid's club.

After we all dutifully nodded and noted, Frank started his prepared spiel. He began with the fact that the area's rich volcanic soil (hence the rust color of the earth) had originally been farmed by the early Hawaiians. A portion of that land was then turned into ranches or sugar cane farms, some of which had stayed in the same families for generations. Nowadays, Upcountry (as Frank told us the area was called) contained a variety of farms growing everything from lavender to strawberries to dragon fruit. It was also, as Frank dutifully let us know, still known for its ranching—even if some of those ranches were now used for things like the winery that would be our last stop of the day—while the majority of the sugar cane farms had been transformed into other uses.

Our first stop was Kapena Ranch. As we pulled through a fence that looked like it had been there 100 years (and probably had been as—according to Frank—the ranch just celebrated its 125th anniversary), the rugged terrain we had been bouncing through opened up to a wide-open pasture with a big red barn and gaggle of waiting horses. Truthfully, it looked more like a scene out of an old Western than what I expected to find in Hawaii. While it was beautiful, the sight of the horses immediately made my palms sweat. As I mentioned, horses have never been my favorite things. Dogs, yes; horses, no.

We were greeted by a striking woman wearing cowboy boots, jeans, and a white shirt featuring the Kapena Ranch logo in what looked like turquoise-colored beading above the pocket. Her long black hair was speckled with streaks of gray and pulled up into a bun with a gorgeous fuchsia flower holding it together. Her age, regal bearing, and flawless ability to accessorize reminded me of Mona, even if their worlds couldn't be farther apart. She stood near ten saddled horses, with a half dozen men in cowboy hats all standing in a row behind her. I wondered if we would continue to have this kind of royal reception everywhere we went (spoiler alert: we did).

"Aloha! Welcome to Kapena Ranch. I'm so glad you could all join us," the woman said. "My name is Kealani. This ranch has been in my family for four generations. We are particularly proud of the fact that through the years, with development all around us, our original ahupua'a has been left intact."

On what I'm sure were more than a few questioning faces, Kealani continued. "An ahupua'a is a type of Hawaiian land division that stretches from the mauka side of the property," Kealani said, gesturing toward the mountain, "to the makai." She gestured down to the ocean. "Essentially, it is a type of use that sustainably supports the land's natural resources, which is something that was important to my great great grandfather, a Scottish sea captain who received the land when he married a member of the Hawaiian royal family—and continues to be important to us today."

Kealani then pointed to the cowboys standing stoically next to the horses. "Our ranch family has also stayed the same. Most of our paniolos, which if you haven't heard yet, is what we call cowboys here in Hawaii, are descendants of the ones who have worked this ranch for generations. While this is still a working cattle ranch, we—after meeting with Clive Kealoha from your hotel—have just started adding these horseback rides. This way we can impart to visitors some of the ways of the paniolos in a manner that is more authentic and respectful of the land and not just tacked on to other activities like the zip lining they offer on the property next to ours."

As Kealani continued her talk, I started eyeing the horses and trying to figure out which one I was going to be riding. As I have mentioned (more than once, I do realize), horses and I had not always been a good match after a bad experience I had in Girl Scouts. And, yes, it is not lost on me that Girl Scouts was not always the morale-boosting experience it was supposed to be. Anyway, the incident (if you will) at the Girl Scout Camp I attended in the Santa Cruz Mountains involved a horse named Red Jet that kept trying to—and ultimately succeeded in—rubbing me off on every tree we passed. I ended up bruised and battered and, since then, haven't been all that keen on the animals.

I tried to keep an open mind but could feel the fear trickling out through my palms, which were already sweating profusely. This horse was not named Red Jet, I reminded myself, and I was not at Girl Scout Camp. No, the horse I was brought over to by the nice paniolo—who said his name was Kekoa—was called Noe (which he pronounced "no-ee").

I gave Noe a tentative pet and then, as Kekoa adjusted the saddle, let him know about my fear of horses. Kekoa, who was tall and had a substantial frame and looked for all the world like he feared nothing, just kept smiling and shaking his head and saying "no trouble" as I babbled on to him with the Girl Scout story. I noticed he wore a fancy belt buckle the size of a frisbee (I might be embellishing that a bit, but it was big) so I asked him about it, and he said—in the same unassuming manner he had just used to introduce himself—that he had won it in the Makawao Stampede, a rodeo that's held every year on the 4th of July. Impressive.

"Okay, Sam, she's ready for you." Kekoa took Noe's reins and brought her over to the step stool to help me climb on. I took in some deep breaths and tried to take myself back to the feeling of relaxation I had during the Lomi Lomi massage to calm myself down.

"Noe is short for Noelani, which means 'heavenly mist,' Sam. She is very gentle. You really do not have to worry."

Kekoa's words were very calming, and I will admit Noe was pretty. She had a gray coat dotted with white freckles and a black mane, and her dark eyes were very kind. I gave her a few more pets to let her know I came in peace before swinging my legs over the saddle and grabbing onto the reins and the saddle horn. I tried not to look to see how the others were doing, so I could concentrate fully on staying upright and therefore not embarrassing myself but couldn't help but take a quick peek.

Fred, still in his tweed jacket, sat languidly in his saddle talking to Brian, also looking quite comfortable. Frank tipped his cap and Brian waved when they saw me turn. I gave a weak little wave and then returned my death grip to the saddle horn before continuing to look around. Mac and Frank were sitting on their horses chatting like old pals, even though I knew they had only met the night before. Trevor looked as scared as I did (thank god!). He was next to Taylor, who look annoyed, but that was kind of her baseline look so it was hard to tell if that was Trevor-related. And Dorothy, tiny Dorothy. She again looked to be in heaven as she sat quite comfortably on her horse and swung this way and that so she could take pictures of all of us and the surroundings with her giant Nikon camera. Dorothy caught me looking her way. I smiled and meekly waved, and she took my picture. Damn her.

Kealani got on her horse—a horse that looked as regal as she did, I noted—and took the lead, with the others all following behind. I was the last of our group to head out, with Kekoa right behind me at the back. We started snaking our way through the ranch and then onto a path that led us into more dense tropical foliage, then along a gulch that was the recipient of water from a gorgeous waterfall high up on the mountain. That's what most people saw, I am pretty sure. I saw glimpses of it, but mostly I saw my hands as they grasped the saddle horn and kept a tight grip on the reins.

When we got to a fork in the road, we turned and started heading up the mountain toward the waterfall. Noe had her ears back and kept bobbling her head and pulling this way and that, which made me pull in the reins even harder to keep her going in a straight line. Soon, when the path got a little wider, Kekoa appeared beside me on his horse.

"Sam, loosen the reins. Noe knows what she's doing. You are new to this path, but she is not, so you have to let go and trust."

Let go and trust? Ha! He obviously didn't know me at all! But since he was still watching me, I started inching my way back on the reins. The more I let go, the more Noe relaxed, and the more Noe relaxed, the more I relaxed. Okay, maybe this was working.

"Very good. Now sit back and enjoy your surroundings, Sam. We are in one of the most beautiful places on earth; you should acknowledge that."

I sat back. Noe didn't bolt but instead perked her ears forward and, in what I have to admit was one of the most gentle walks I had ever experienced, continued to meander her way along the path through the tropical paradise. We had a stream on our right and a waterfall up ahead, and okay, life was pretty good.

"Thank you, Kekoa."

"A'ole pilikia, Sam."

"Ah-oh-leh pee-lee-kee-yah?" I said, sounding out phonetically what I thought he said.

"That's right."

"What does that mean?"

103

"It means you are welcome, or like a lot of the kids today say, 'no problem.'"

"And how do I say thank you?"

"Mahalo."

"Mahalo, Kekoa."

"A'ole pilikia, Sam."

I smiled and noticed that I was hardly holding onto Noe at all anymore. As Kekoa had promised, she knew just where to go as we gently followed the others along the path, and I reveled in the beauty surrounding me. At one point, I noticed there was a break in the greenery on my right and peeked over and saw what appeared to be a clearing with a large house or even a compound.

"What's in there?"

"A friend's house."

"A friend."

"He prefers not to be identified."

Oooo. Secret. I like secrets and decided I might have to do a little investigating if I ever got the chance. Instead, we continued looping over to our left and started to begin our descent. I could see the red barn of the ranch in the distance and realized the ride was actually almost over. When we arrived back at the stables, Brittany was waiting for us, and I realized she hadn't gone on the ride at all even though she had been wearing her riding boots earlier at the hotel. While we were gone, she had changed and was now dressed for the rest of the day in a sundress and sassy sandals and waving to us on our return.

"I hope you all had an amazing time!" Brittany said as we each pulled up to the step stool to disembark from our horses. "We have about 15 minutes before we need to leave for our next destination, so if you need to use the restroom or, as I mentioned, would like to change out of your jeans and close-toed shoes, feel free to use the bathrooms in the barn. In the meantime, I'm sure you would all like to thank Kealani and her team for the wonderful and oh-so-special treat."

Okay, so I guess it was a pretty special treat, but since my feet were not on the ground yet, I was withholding my judgment. Finally, Kekoa helped me off Noe. I gave both of them a very nice "Mahalo" for taking such good care of me, thanked Kealani, and followed the others into the barn. So, yeah, it was a somewhat enjoyable experience, but I was still glad I wouldn't have to repeat the equine experience again for a long, long time. Or so I thought.

CHAPTER NINE

Once the adrenaline of the horseback ride wore off and I had swapped my jeans and tennies for capris and sandals, the rest of the day was a bit of a blur. We would all troop in and out of the van to find a gaggle of smiling people waiting to give us a spiel about their particular property and then a sample of whatever tour or activity they offered. Because of our time constraints, these were all speed versions of their usual offerings, which meant a lot more of them telling us what guests could expect than us actually getting to experience it all ourselves. At least we'd gotten that horseback ride in, right? Ha.

We were handed press kits (and often a little gift) at each stop, but I still made sure to take constant pictures on my iPhone and write down anything interesting in the notes so I could remember the details when it was time to actually write the story. I also started talking to the people on the trip I hadn't gotten to really meet yet—just in case one of them had something to do with Alistair's death.

Our first stop was Surfing Goat Dairy, which wasn't far from the ranch. (I think it took longer for us to troop on and off the van than it did to make the drive.) There, we were immediately greeted by a gaggle of baby goats (by far the cutest of the greeting parties) along with a young gal named Beatrice. She said the owners were out of town, but she would be happy to take us on a quick tour of the farm and cheese tasting. That last part was exciting to hear as I was starting to get hungry after skipping breakfast and getting my heart rate up so high on that darn horseback ride.

I walked around the grounds of the farm and pet the baby goats with Brian, who I learned had indeed been a football player—offensive lineman—at Northwestern University (hence the t-shirt he was wearing) before busting a knee and getting his master's degree in journalism. As Fred had alluded, Brian was a contributing editor for a magazine called *Meetings Now*. He filled me in on the meetings-and-events part of the larger travel industry, which it ended up was huge—especially for hotels—as meeting planners book a LOT of hotel rooms. Brian lived in the Chicago area, where a lot of the medical associations are based, and said he also did a lot of consulting with organizations on their events. When I told Brian I lived in Carmel and had recently toured the Monterey Conference Center, he said he was out there at least once a year as his doctors' groups were big on golfing at Pebble Beach. We made plans to meet up the next time that happened.

All interesting stuff but it didn't tell me anything about his relationship with Alistair. During the cheese tasting (hallelujah—and yum!), I finally found my chance to ask Brian about that. We were seated at small tables in an open-air room with tiny tastes placed before us of the more than 20 different varieties of goat cheese the farm produced along with crackers, olives, pickles, and nuts. I started in with Brian the same way I had with Fred at the luau.

"This is all so weird about Alistair, huh?"

Brian shrugged. "I guess. But, let's face it, the guy had issues."

"In what way?"

"The usual for a man his age who lived the way he did."

"Too much eating and drinking?"

"Definitely that but also just, well, his anger at everything."

"What do you mean?"

"It's like the man never stopped, you know?"

"Stopped what?"

Brian pondered for a second as we both tasted the "Maui's Secret" cheese, which we were informed was a creamy cheese aged in their own roasted garlic olive oil with hints of lemon zest and thyme. Brian pointed the cheese with a nod of enjoyment.

"My wife would love this," he said.

I smiled and nodded, then prodded again. "You said Alistair never stopped?"

"Trying to muscle his way through the world. I'm not sure what he thought he would win by knocking everyone out of his way, but he made sure to do that at every turn."

"You had a history with him?"

"Not too much. Enough."

"Fred said something about a train ride?"

Brian gave Fred a look, maybe a little perturbed he'd been talking about him, then shrugged. "Yeah. I forgot Fred was there. It was a press trip on the Rocky Mountaineer in Western Canada. Great train ride and very popular with groups, so I was covering it for the magazine. From the very first night, we all realized how awful Alistair was and did our best to avoid him. Pretty easy on a train. He sits down, one by one we'd all move to other parts of the train. You know the drill."

I nodded.

"There was also a lot of jockeying of position for the best seat in the dome coach—the one that's all glass so you can get the best views and, hence, best pictures." He gestured to the other writers around us. "As you have probably learned, that's a big thing with everyone on these trips."

Again, I nodded.

"I had snagged the perfect seat just as we were about to go by some of the highest peaks in the Canadian Rockies—gorgeous stuff—and he brings the porter over and loudly announces that I had stolen his seat."

"He can't do that, can he?"

"He did. I was the only Black guy on the trip, too. Kind of like this one," Brian said, looking around. "That's not always the case—especially with meeting planner FAMs—but it happens enough that when it does, I know I'm representing more than just the travel industry, you know?"

"I'm sorry. It shouldn't be that way."

"It is what it is, Sam, especially when you are a guy my size. You deal. So, I did. I sublimated a desire to clock the guy and, instead, stood up, said 'my mistake' and left to join the rest of the group. They had all already departed for the bar car when they saw Alistair approaching. I had been so immersed in the scenery I hadn't noticed. Luckily, I was able to snap enough pictures for my story—and the public relations people had some gorgeous stock images as well—that it was fine. But I did learn to avoid him at all costs, both on that trip and a few others I found myself on with him."

"That's why you were at the other table at the opening reception?"

"You betcha. Dorothy and I go way back, so once we saw the table he had chosen, we managed to stay as far away from him as possible that night."

"Smart."

"Wasn't born yesterday." He looked at me. "Sorry, didn't mean to insinuate you were."

"Hey, I get it, I'm a newbie—at least when it comes to this stuff." I waved my hand indicating all that was around us.

"Not bad, huh?"

"Not bad at all."

"We are definitely treated well. In general, it's not a bad business to be in."

"Fred said something similar."

"Fred would know. He's been doing it longer than any of us."

Brian again nodded over at Fred, who saw us and nodded back from across the room and lifted his cheese-filled cracker in a toast. Brian smiled and lifted his back and then winced a little.

"Are you hurt?"

"Nothing major," Brian said. "Just a cut. One of the lamps in my room had a sharp edge that I caught the side of my hand on when I went to turn it on."

Before I had a chance to ask what the lamp looked like, we saw Brittany waving from across the room near the van. Brian saw her. "There she is. Our drill sergeant keeping us on schedule."

"Is she typical in terms of the type of person leading these trips?"

"Yes and no. They're usually on the young side like she is, but some are savvier than others," he said, nodding in Brittany's direction and grinning.

We headed back into the van and drove over to Ocean Vodka. On that tour, a young man who introduced himself as one of the family members that owned the distillery gave us the spiel: How, on their 80 acres, they grew more than 30 varieties of organic sugar cane and then distilled it on-site using desalinated deep ocean mineral water they brought in from off the coast of Hawaii Island (aka the Big Island).

I chose Mac as my partner during our tour of the sugar cane farm, distillery, and bottling plant. As we walked through the farm, I noticed his pink skin was getting even pinker in the midday sun. I let him know, and he pulled out the Mokihana Resort & Spa cap that had been left in our rooms the night before.

"They're nice, huh?" I said, pointing to the cap, as we walked into the distillery and bottling plant.

"Totally," said Mac.

"This is my first press trip, so I'm still getting used to the idea that gifts will be left in my room every night."

"Pretty rad, right?"

"Totally rad," I said, with a straight face (I hoped). "Have you been doing this long? No offense, but you seem a lot younger than the others."

He shrugged. "That's usually the case. It used to be worse. I've been helping my Uncle Bob out on his magazine since my summers in college. Then I was always the youngest. But it's cool. I like old people."

Ouch. I let it go. "What magazine is that?"

"It's called *Adventure Man*. It's actually pretty cool—cars and gear and travel and stuff like that. Uncle Bob worked for *Outside* in the early days. Then he broke off to start his own magazine. It's not nearly as big as *Outside*. Geared more to older guys who might not be as active as those dudes, but maybe have a little more money. They like their gadgets and, you know, prefer staying in a resort after a day of adventure instead of roughing it."

"You describe it very well."

"That's just the short version. Uncle Bob sends the whole extended family on trips for the magazine. Helps him keep the name out there, and we all get cool trips. Win-win, right? We all get the speech beforehand on how to 'position' the magazine."

"I got that speech from my editor."

"So, you know the drill. He used to make me carry actual magazines to hand out on trips. That was a drag. They're heavy, you know? Now that it's mostly all online I just make sure all the people in the places I visit know it still exists. Then when I get home, I write up a story and add my photos, and boom, Uncle Bob has new copy on the site."

"Is this what you do full-time?"

"No. Uncle Bob doesn't even pay us. It's how he stays in business," he said, laughing. "We do it for the perks. I mean, this is pretty rad, right?"

"Totally rad." Again, I tried to sound serious so Mac wouldn't think I was mocking him. And I wasn't. Really.

"What do you do when you aren't traveling for your uncle, then?"

"Art's my real bag. It's what I studied at UC Santa Cruz. Now I live at an artist cooperative in this humongous warehouse in Oakland. There's a lead dude there that the rest of us help create these ginormous art installations for Burning Man. Like last year ours was the one with the giant spider caught in its own web. You may have seen it there."

I laughed at the fact he thought I might ever attend Burning Man but just shook my head. "Sorry, wasn't there last year."

"It was rad."

"So, did you know Alistair?"

"Who's that?"

"The guy who died."

"Ha. No. Thought you might be talking about someone at Burning Man. Never met the dude, but I had definitely heard stories about him from Uncle Bob. Bummer him croaking and all, though, huh?"

"Definite bummer."

By this point, we were walking out of the building that held the distillery and bottling line and into their new cafe, which the owner pointed out to Brian was available for group events. Just like the goat cheese farm, our tour would end with a tasting, but this time it was vodka and various cocktails created to show off the vodka. As we entered the cafe, we saw them all lined up on the bar.

"Rad," said Mac.
"Totally rad, Mac. Totally rad."

CHAPTER TEN

S oon it was back into the van for the drive over to the Ali'i Kula Lavender Farm for a tour and a late lunch (thank god for the goat cheese, which not only helped tide me over hunger-wise but also soaked some of up the vodka). After taking the requisite tour through the lavender fields by a young gal in a breezy sundress, we were led to some tables with benches. There, we were instructed on how to make wreaths out of lavender and other flowers. During the wreath-making and lunch, I sat next to Dorothy, who I have to say was just so much fun. What a complete change from the first night when she was cowering away from Alistair with the group at the other table. She still had her huge Nikon with her, so I asked about it. She told me she got her start as a photojournalist during the Vietnam War.

Her love of travel helped her transition into travel writing, but she never completely gave up her photography and even still had the occasional gallery show.

Dorothy had some amazing stories about the early days of her career and the adventures she had been on that had me laughing hysterically. She told me the industry had changed a lot with the addition of the bloggers and influencers but that it wasn't necessarily a bad thing as her own travel blog still gave her a regular outlet. That gave me my in to ask about Alistair.

"I heard he was responsible for you losing some of your regular outlets."

Dorothy sighed. "Yes. That's true. I had already been on the scene for a while when he was starting to make his way in the industry. He always kind of resented that I had the better assignments—in those days sometimes I had multiple publications that wanted stories from the same trip."

"Multiple assignments? How does that work?"

"When I was invited on a trip, I would send the invitation to all my regular outlets and ask if they might be interested in a story. As a free-lancer, I'm not representing a particular publi-cation as much the ability to place the story in multiple ones."

"Seems like the hotels and destinations would love that."

"They do if you have a proven track record at placing stories or at least one confirmed assignment. As a staffer, you know you can place the story, but it's just one story in one magazine— maybe a couple if you can use the information later in a trend or theme piece. As a freelancer, it's not as direct a line to publication, but I do try to have at least one guaranteed assignment when I accept a trip. There were times it was multiple. For instance, I was able to write dozens of different stories from a trip that toured the locations used in the "Harry Potter" movies. That one was very popular. On the flip side, I once wrote a wonderful story on how to get the most out of a summer Yellowstone vacation. Then a series of wildfires broke out the week the story was scheduled to run so the editor killed it. Well, not completely killed, but it didn't run until the following year. I've never had a trip that I couldn't write about somewhere, but sometimes it's not as quickly as the public relations people might like."

"Sounds great."

"Well, it was."

"What happened?"

"Two things. One, the recession in the early 2000s hit the newspaper and magazine world hard. A lot folded and never came back. Plus, there was, well…"

"Alistair?"

"Yes, how would you know?"

"Fred mentioned he had done something horrible to you."

Dorothy sighed. "Yeah, it was pretty despicable."

"What happened?"

"I got a great assignment. Really cool one. One of my editors wanted me to photograph and write up a series of castles-turned-hotels that had just opened in Scotland. They included one Alistair really wanted to visit. Alistair desperately wanted that assignment, even though he isn't—wasn't—even a real photographer and that was part of the assignment. He claimed he could find a local photographer at each stop. I'm not sure how he even heard they were planning the story—probably from one of the hotel people—but he kept after the editor to get her to give him the assignment. She refused and he never forgave me for losing out on the story."

"That's so ridiculous."

Dorothy shrugged. "A few years after that my husband got sick, so I had to turn down a few assignments. Alistair pounced, and when my husband died and I started traveling again, he made sure I never got those cush assignments again."

"How did he do that?"

"Made up stories about my lack of professionalism on trips and stuff like that."

"Oh, Dorothy, I'm so sorry."

"I made peace with it a long time ago. It's okay. I still get the occasional invitation based on my history, the little travel blog I started, and my SATW membership…"

"SATW?"

"Society of American Travel Writers."

"There's so much I still don't know about this business."

"You'll learn, dear. You'll learn," Dorothy said, patting my knee. "Anyway, between that and being able to write pieces for the retirement community newsletter where I live in Santa Fe, I find ways to make sure the trip gets at least some coverage. It's just not the same as the airline magazines, national publications, and newspapers where I used to be able to place stories. Alistair knew that and used to use it against me."

"In what way?"

She laughed. "One night when he'd had too much to drink, he said he would blackball me unless I sent him any gifts I received when we were on trips together. They have mostly been the SATW-sponsored trips, which are a little more clubby, so I just did it and it wasn't that big of a deal. I really don't need more stuff, and I hadn't been on a regular press trip with him in years. I saw his name on the itinerary for this trip and figured I should continue the practice, so when the bellman showed up at the door, I told him I preferred that Alistair get my basket. Pretty stupid, right?"

"Stupid and so so petty."

"Petty was Alistair's middle name."

"Ha—that's exactly what Fred said."

"I'm sure he has plenty of his own stories."

As she said this, I realized Fred hadn't really told me any of his own stories.

"But, hey," Dorothy continued, her eyes brightening, "I'm still traveling the world and staying in amazing hotels and meeting lovely people like you, Samantha, which is a lot better than being a widow sitting at home on the couch feeling sorry for myself."

I wanted to pull her tiny body into the biggest hug possible. Instead, I looked down and noticed that she had managed to create a gorgeous wreath out of the herbs and flowers we'd been given. Mine looked more like a bird's nest that had been hit by a hurricane.

"You are amazing with those flowers, Dorothy."

"I've worked with flowers and plants my whole life."

"In what way?"

"Mostly gardening. My garden is where I spend most of my time when I'm home in Santa Fe."

"That's nice. My mom was a florist."

"How wonderful. You didn't follow that path?"

I pointed to the mash of foliage that constituted my "wreath." "Not exactly my strong suit, but we have managed to keep the garden she created at home going."

"That's a wonderful tribute to her. I'm sure she's very proud of you."

Now I did pull her into a one-armed hug and then looked over to find Brittany giving us the signal that it was time to go again.

121

Our final stop dropped us up at the winery in Ulupalakua, which had a gorgeous three-sided view of the ocean that included the south coast, where we could see the Mokihana Resort & Spa. There was a definite chill in the air at that elevation, something I enjoyed, having come from a place where the temperature is close to 60 degrees year-round. For the first time that day, I was glad I'd kept a light jacket tied around my waist (a habit from home) to pull on.

The winery, we learned, was actually on another of Maui's early ranches. As part of the spiel from one of the members of our greeting party, we learned that at one point the ranch had been 40,000 acres but that 20,000 of those acres had been turned over to the State of Hawaii to be preserved as parkland. Known as the Rose Ranch in the late 1800s, it was a favorite of King Kalakaua, and we were told a special cabin had been built for the king and his royal party. That building they now used for the winery, which was added in the 1970s when the ranch returned to its original name of Ulupalakua.

By the time we all trooped over to the tasting room/royal cabin, everybody was pretty loose. Adding wine to our day filled with goat cheese, vodka, and lavender made the conversations louder and more boisterous. It wasn't the best wine I'd ever tasted (at least compared to the local California wines I'd grown up around), but by that point and with that view, it didn't really matter. There was a lot of giggling and even Brittany was starting to let go of the clenched jaw she'd been carrying around all day. Truth be told, with all the conviviality around me, it was almost hard to remember that one of our group had just died.

Soon we were scooted back to the van and heading down the winding road to the hotel. I was seated next to Brittany. I'd actually been sitting next to her the whole day. One of the new press trip things I learned is that—much like the days on the school bus—once someone chooses a seat, it ended up being "their" seat the rest of the day. People kept gravitating back to the seat they first chose and then left all the paraphernalia we picked up along the way: Kapena Ranch backpacks, Surfing Goat coffee mugs, small airplane-sized bottles of Ocean Vodka, and Ali'i Kula Lavender wreaths.

The good thing about sitting next to Brittany was I could pick her brain a bit while also surreptitiously reading the texts she had coming in from Philippa and Brandon, who had stayed back at the resort. Conversation-wise, it took a while to get past the perky PR facade. On the initial ride to the ranch, it was still early, and everyone was quiet and listening to Frank give his spiel, so I stayed mum while she kept click click clicking on her phone.

After the ranch, Brittany was a little more chatty but still all business—the business of marketing the resort. She gave me a full rundown on the chef as we were headed to the goat cheese farm.

"Isn't Chef Marc great? I'm so glad you got to meet him as he does a fabulous job. He came from the Ritz-Carlton Grand Cayman and on his very first day here made it a point to partner with all the local farmers, including those we're going to meet today. I mean, did you try that lavender goat cheese at the luau? Just scrumptious and you'll see why when we get there next."

This was all spilling out of her mouth while Frank was giving more of the history of Upcountry farming and she was simultaneously clicking away on her phone. I have to admit it was some truly impressive multi-tasking. From what I could see, it appeared there was a group text chain with her and Philippa and Brandon and maybe some other hotel people I didn't know. Among the things they discussed was the fact that Brittany would need to let the travel agency know that our return flights would all have to be changed.

On the ride between the goat cheese farm and the vodka distillery, Brittany moved on to essentially repeating everything I had already read in the bios in the kit I received when I arrived at the hotel: "… and the management team is really top-notch. Philippa is just a gem. A gem. She's kind of a role model, don't you think? Just so elegant. She has really raised the service level at the resort and is the one who brought on Brandon. He's been a wonderful addition—not to mention not bad on the eyes—am I right?"

She turned her own baby blues in my direction, and it occurred to me they would make a very attractive couple, even if she was a good decade younger than he was. Her phone buzzed and she looked down at a new missive in the group text. It appeared to be something about what time the Haleakala bike company would be picking everyone up for the ride the next day. She texted back "3 a.m." I almost yelped but held back so she wouldn't know I was reading them.

After the vodka tour—where I noticed she had downed quite a few of the "tastes" we were given—Brittany started opening up a little.

"I just can't believe I was so stupid to invite Alistair," she confided. "I mean, death aside, you know?" I gave her my most sympathetic nod. "I knew the stories. I knew what he was capable of and that he might ruin the trip for everyone, but I really thought I could charm him into behaving..."

I wasn't sure what to say so, again, I just nodded sympathetically.

"Hubris, right?" she asked and then the phone beeped again. A text popped up saying that Detective Kai was back at the hotel again, this time visiting Alistair's room. Now, that was interesting.

After the lavender farm, she was back on message. "Isn't Frank adorable? He's done a great job with the kid's club and working with Clive to add more cultural components and activities like these to the offerings at the resort. They're even looking to add a surf butler. Wouldn't that be fun?"

Her smile quickly dissolved when the ping from the phone went off again. It looked to be something about Detective Kai talking to their head of security. Then, on the ride back down the hill, another text came in. By then, she was starting to nod off, but I could see in the preview of the message something about Detective Kai finding a glitch in the security tapes—yes, the very same security tapes that had me as the last person to enter Alistair's room.

Now that was really interesting....

CHAPTER ELEVEN

W e were back at the hotel by 6 p.m. They gave us a free evening since we had that darn 3 a.m. call for our Haleakala Sunrise Bike Tour. I know, 3 a.m., right? Crazy. At least I could console myself with the fact I was getting up at that godforsaken hour for a work-related activity. The idea that people actually booked these tours for fun kind of boggled my mind. I guess I'd soon learn just how worthy of the early start it could be.

As I started down the hall toward my room, admittedly still a little tipsy from the wine tasting, I decided to walk the seven rooms past to take a look at Alistair's suite. All those texts coming in on Brittany's phone had gotten my curiosity up. Yellow police tape covered the double doors of the suite. I looked across the hall and found the security camera—the one that recorded my visit two nights earlier—tucked into a corner. When I looked back, I noticed the door with the keyhole wasn't completely closed.

Wondering if Detective Kai was still inside, I tapped on the door a bit and it swung open. Really, it did. Just swung open.

"Hello?" I called out. "Detective Kai? Anybody here?" See? I was being good.

It seemed silly for me not to go in with the door just hanging open, so I tiptoed into the suite with a strange sense of déjà vu from having been there two nights earlier. From what I could see as I scanned the room, everything looked the same. I again noticed just how ridiculously humongous the suite was compared to my own guest room, which could fit into the living room portion located to the right as I came through the door.

The living room didn't seem to have been touched at all, so I turned toward the dining room and then to the bar area immediately to my left. I noticed that the Koa wood lamp I had looked at that was on the bar was now lying on the ground and had been marked by a police flat with the number 12. I was smart enough not to touch it— although it occurred to me that it had most likely been already dusted, and my fingerprints were probably on it from the night I was there.

I continued my scan of the bar area and noticed that the ice bucket was still there (although the ice itself and the bottle of Veuve Clicquot were gone) and that there were still two amenity baskets next to it filled with fruit juices, muffins, and tropical flowers. Now that I knew that one of them was Dorothy's, I could see it still had a small card with her name on it tucked into the top. That one looked untouched, but in the other basket, the muffin tops were missing and a few of the juice bottles were half full—exactly as I remembered them looking the other night. There was something else about the arrangement that looked different. I couldn't quite put my finger on it, so I took my iPhone out and took a picture of each basket to take a closer look later.

I then backtracked to the ice bucket and again noticed the leather portfolio with Alistair's name engraved on the cover sitting next to it. This time I could see there was a Four Seasons Hotels & Resorts logo embossed on the cover—another gift from a hotel, I assumed. I pulled the sleeves of my jacket over my fingers to open it since I hadn't touched it on that first night. On the top, I recognized the press trip itinerary, on which he had written some notes on the hotel that Brittany would be happy to see were relatively positive. Behind that were printouts of some of his clips. Seriously, who carries their clips around with them? This was especially true these days when everything is digital, although a few looked pretty old (as in pre-digital). One was from a *USA Today* newspaper article and had the headline "Hotel Opening Goes Awry in Southwest." I wondered if he'd just brought it to torture Brittany in some way since he had mentioned that hotel in Taos at the opening reception. I squinted to see if she was among the group of people in the photo, but it was so small and faded it was impossible to make out. Still, there was something about it that was triggering something in the back of my brain … but just as I was about to read further, I heard a serious sigh coming from the doorway.

"Ms. Powers, what are you doing here?"

I turned to find Detective Kai standing in the doorway looking very unhappy with me. I did not like that look. Not at all.

"The door was open," I said. "I swear."

"The police tape didn't give you any pause?"

"Well, I thought I might find you in here," I said. "And I thought I should maybe share some of the things I learned today."

"We will be talking, but I'm afraid now we will have to do it down at the station."

Now that I really didn't like…

Okay, so this was definitely not the relaxation room in the spa at the Mokihana Resort. As the daughter of someone who worked his way up through a series of law enforcement jobs on the Monterey Peninsula, I had spent more than my fair share of time in police stations and jails. Heck, I used to do my homework in a room almost identical to the interrogation room Detective Kai drove me to in silence and then deposited me in for a few hours with not even my phone to occupy me due to the lack of Wifi or cell reception.

Punishment, I suppose, for crossing the police tape and entering Alistair's suite.

In order not to go insane, I started to think about how I would review this room compared to the others (other interrogation rooms, not luxury resort spa relaxation rooms). It was, well, about the same. The tropical locale of the police station didn't really change the fact that the room had the same four gray walls, metallic table, and chairs that were de rigueur in these settings. Made me wonder if there was a design guide for jails with notes like "metallic gray and the lack of any visual stimuli really bring out the honesty in those you are interrogating."

I would have to ask Uncle Henry when I got home. Ugh. Henry was going to be PISSED that I had been brought in for tampering with evidence. If they actually booked me, I would have to call him and could already hear the disappointment dripping from his response when I told him what was going on.

Luckily, Detective Kai interrupted this reverie of disappointment by entering the room. Then he gave me his own look of disappointment. Oh, come on.

"Ms. Powers."

"Detective."

"You know why you are here, right?"

"I suppose."

"And do you have anything to say about it?"

Actually, it suddenly occurred to me that I did. "So, you brought me in for, what, possibly tampering with the evidence?"

"Let's say you're right."

"That must mean that a crime was committed."

"I'm sorry?"

"What I am hearing you tell me is that Alistair the Ascot…"

"Alistair the what?"

"Oh, sorry, that's what I called him in my head because he wore that silly ascot—you know, the scarf around his neck—at the opening reception. I mean, we're in Hawaii on the beach, and he's got his neck all wrapped up. I get that it's his, you know, 'look' or 'brand' [yes, I added the air quotes; Chelsea would be proud of me] but, really … on the beach … in Hawaii…"

"Got it."

"Anyway, what I'm hearing you tell me is that Alistair didn't die of natural causes. Otherwise, no evidence could be tampered with and therefore why all the fuss?"

I got a head tilt from him. It was slight but discernible.

"So, he was murdered? Wow! That would actually be quite shocking, wouldn't it? My first press trip and someone was actually murdered," I said. "It's very Agatha Christie, don't you think, except we aren't on a train and are in, you know, Hawaii…"

"I would appreciate it if you wouldn't say anything to the others about the possible cause of death."

"Well, I still don't know the possible cause of death, but I get you. As you so diligently pointed out when we first met, I grew up in a law enforcement household and have written a lot about crime so I can be cool. Really, I can."

"Glad you can be cool." He smiled (an actual smile!) as he said that, and I noticed again —yes, even under the circumstances—that he really was quite handsome. I had to squelch a desire to ruffle the perfect military-style brush cut he had to his hair.

"Totally. Cool." Okay, we were talking about a man being murdered, and I was being a bit cheeky. Again—as my dad and my uncle and even my former editor at the *Times* could attest—snarky humor and inappropriate thoughts (like ruffling military brush cuts in a police station) were my default coping mechanism when put in uncomfortable situations like, you know, learning a man I had just met might have been murdered.

Kai wasn't smiling anymore. "I do hope you understand this is a serious situation, Ms. Powers."

I put my hands out in a peace offering. "Sorry. It's just all a bit overwhelming, you know?"

"I can imagine," he said, looking at his notes. "Now, you mentioned having some information to share."

"Yes! Well, that kind of depends. I mean, how was he killed? How do you know it was murder?"

"Might be."

"How do you know it might be murder and he didn't just, say, bump his noggin on the Jacuzzi?"

This got his attention. "How do you know that he had a head trauma?"

I figured there was no reason to lie, so I pointed to his notes. "I read it in your notes when you interviewed me the other day."

He instinctively covered his notes up a bit with the legal pad. "Impressive, but it ends up that wasn't the cause of death."

"It wasn't? So, he just bumped it on the way down and something else caused it? Or, I don't know, someone didn't know he was dead—or dying—and bopped him on the head? Again, I don't mean to sound disrespectful."

Kai didn't nod but he didn't deny it either. Interesting. Then it again occurred to me.

"So, unless you were coming to take the crime scene tape down—and, as I mentioned, in that case, why would I be here—he didn't have, say, a natural heart attack and hit his head falling from that, either."

I sat back, feeling rather smug. Kai thought for a moment before speaking.

"It's inconclusive."

"Inconclusive?"

"Inconclusive."

Now, that was interesting—both that he was kind of actually talking to me about the case and that they didn't really know the cause of death. Or, at least, that's what I thought he was saying. "You're saying the cause of death was inconclusive?"

"His heart stopped. That much we know. And it wasn't caused by—as you so colorfully put it—getting bopped on the head. Whether the heart stopping was natural or, well, induced is what we need further tests to confirm."

Induced? "So, you are conducting those further tests?"

"Yes. The medical examiner feels that there is something there—something that, let's say, helped the heart to stop. We just don't know what."

Interesting. "Interesting," I said. "So, then the bop could be a natural effect of falling. Or it could have come from someone who wanted to make sure that the induced heart attack took, as it were."

"As it were." Detective Kai smiled but then became more serious. "But I must reiterate, this is not your case to cover or to solve. I know you are used to being in the middle of things, Ms. Powers…"

"Please. Sam."

"But Sam, this is not your case," he said.

"You would still like to hear what I learned, though, wouldn't you, Detective Kai?"

"You can call me Roger. And, sure, what have you got?"

Roger. I suppressed a giggle at the fact he had the same name as Lizzy and my's favorite tennis player: Roger Federer. He really did get cuter by the minute, but don't worry, I stayed focused.

"Roger, I'm sure you noticed there were two amenity baskets." Another nod. "And that the second one had Dorothy's name on it?" Nod. "I guess it's something he's been doing for years—having her send him the gifts she receives in exchange for not blabbing the fact she's not writing for any big publications anymore."

Roger wrote Dorothy's name down.

"Not that I think she had anything to do with this," I continued. "She's really a lovely person and the truth is it ends up almost everyone in the press group had some sort of beef with Alistair."

More note taking. "Even the hotel people were not fans, as far as I could see," I said. "For one, he made them upgrade his room to a suite."

"You mentioned that when we first met."

"Yes, and he hounded that poor Brittany until the hotel sent a bottle of Veuve Clicquot to his room—speaking of which, did you remove that from the room?"

He ignored me. "I'm still not hearing anything worth poisoning him for."

"Poison, eh? Well, guess it would have to be some kind of poison, huh? Was it the Veuve? Again, I noticed it was missing. Did you test it?"

"It wasn't the champagne."

"Huh. And nobody but me showed up on the security tapes going into his room that night?"

"They're a bit inconclusive as well."

"What? They're inconclusive?"

"Sorry. I have said too much. Again, Sam, this is not your case," said Roger. "What I really need is for you to rejoin the group back at the Mokihana Resort and let us investigate. Okay?"

"Okay."

"No going into his room. No investigating on your own."

"Fine."

Okay, I may have had my fingers crossed for that one.

CHAPTER TWELVE

etective Kai—aka my new pal Roger—drove me back to the hotel. Since I knew from the ride out that it was going to be a good half hour to get from the police department in Wailuku back to the resort in the Wailea development on the south shore, I attempted to make small talk. I did this partly as a way to stay awake since I had now been up almost all night and also because I have to admit the detective intrigued me.

"Nice car." I know, lame start, but you try making small talk after a full day of activities and no sleep.

"Thanks."

"A Honda Pilot isn't exactly what I'd expect to see a cop driving."

"It's actually my own car. The department sub-sidizes the cars the detectives drive, but they have to come from a list of approved vehicles. Then they set it up with the lights and radio and other department specifics."

Oh, yeah, this was one scintillating conversation.

"Interesting," I lied.

"Not really." He laughed, which made me laugh.

"No, not really." I then again noticed the leather cords he had wrapped around his wrist. It appeared there were four of them. Each consisted of a series of braided leather strands with small clasps that all looked to be in different shapes. A fishhook and a turtle were the ones I could make out. It was hard to see the others. "What's with those?" I said, pointing to his wrist.

"What?"

"The bracelets?"

"What about them?"

"They seem a little off-brand."

"Off-brand?"

"Yeah, I know. Kill me now for using that phrase but, you know, everything else about you screams, well, 'cop' and then you've got these leather bands around your wrist that say something else."

"What exactly do you think they say?"

"That there's a wild side to you, Detective Roger Kai."

He laughed. "A wild side, huh?"

I shrugged. "Could be."

He smiled but continued driving without saying anything. Now I was even more curious, but since he wasn't revealing any more information, I let it go.

Soon, Roger was pulling into the porte-cochere to drop me off. The sky was just starting to get a little lighter in preparation for the sunrise. It reminded me that I was missing the bike ride down Haleakala.

"Shoot. I missed the departure for the bike ride."

"Yeah. Sorry about that. I let the hotel team know that we had some questions for you and that you wouldn't be able to attend this morning's activity."

"Thanks. I guess."

"Maybe next time you will think twice about breaking and entering."

"I still contend there was no breaking involved. Entering, okay, yeah, you got me."

He smiled. "Get some sleep, Sam."

"You, too, Roger."

He drove off and I walked into the lobby, where I noted again that the view never failed to impress no matter the time of day or night. As the marble started to glow with the rising of the sun, I pictured the press group happily descending the curving road down from the volcano with envy. I stopped at the same cart I had the day before for a coffee and a smoothie. Simone (still from Harrisburg, Pennsylvania) asked if I wanted them made the same as I had the previous day. Wow, was that only a day before? So much had happened.

As I waited for the drinks, I looked down at my phone. Naturally, there was a text waiting from Brittany about my not making the bike ride. She said that Detective Kai had let them know that they were speaking to me so hadn't waited (phew) and that she was disappointed I was missing the adventure but would see me at our dinner event. It was pretty amazing how I could feel her stress levels rising even through the text.

I went back to my room and stood on my balcony looking out at the gorgeous sunrise and contemplated all that had happened in the past three days. I figured I might as well start going through the pictures from our Upcountry day and post them on the *Carmel Today* sites before getting some sleep. I went back in and sat at the well-appointed desk and opened my computer to allow the photos to sync from the camera in my phone.

Once they were all up, I pulled out photos from the horseback ride, the vodka-making tour, the goat cheese and lavender farms, and the winery. Lots of shots of happy people enjoying the simple pleasures of Maui life. #CarmelToday #GoMaui #UpcountryMaui etc. etc.

As I went through the photographs, I got to the ones I had taken in Alistair's suite before I was so rudely interrupted by Detective Kai. The pictures of the bar area included Alistair's monogrammed portfolio containing the note-filled itinerary and the two baskets. They were identical, except that Alistair's had been picked through. The muffin tops were all missing, as was one of the fruit drinks. But again, there was something else. The more I looked, the more I realized they weren't completely identical.

I compared the photo to the basket in my room and noticed my basket was closer in looks to Dorothy's—mainly because I hadn't really had time to eat anything except for one of the muffins and Alistair had really kind of ravaged through his. Dorothy's was, of course, untouched. But there was something else. Maybe it had to do with the flowers, which were a bit different in all of our baskets—but what did I know about tropical flowers, right? I knew someone who did, though, and placed a call to my Uncle Henry.

At this point, it was still only 6 a.m. my time but that meant it was about 8 a.m. in Carmel—or maybe 9 a.m. There are times of the year when Hawaii is two hours earlier than the Pacific Time Zone and times when it is three (because Hawaii doesn't go on Daylight Savings Time). I could never remember which was which. Either way, Uncle Henry would be up. As I looked at the palm trees outside my window, I pictured Uncle Henry, coffee cup in hand, sitting in his chair in the living room and reading the newspaper with Buster beside him and a view of the Monterey cypress, my mom's succulent garden, and the ocean beyond.

"Sam!" he answered. "So good to hear from you."

"Good to hear your voice as well. How's Dad?"

"He's fine. They have someone taking him on a walk down to the beach every day and he is loving that." He paused for a second, acknowledging the guilt we still both felt at not having been able to handle his illness ourselves. "He's not unhappy."

"I know. I'm glad all is well."

"How is Hawaii? I've enjoyed following your adventures on the *Carmel Today* website."

"Thanks, Uncle Henry. Adventure is the operative word."

"How so?"

"Well, one of the writers on the trip dropped dead."

"I'm sorry?"

"Dead. And while they're not sure quite yet how he died—except that, you know, his heart stopped—it looks suspicious."

"A suspicious death on a trip. Very Agatha Christie, except for the Hawaiian setting, of course."

"That's what I said! So, here's the thing: I kind of snuck into the victim's room last night..."

"Oh, Sam, you didn't."

"I did. Hey, the door was ajar, and I was walking right by. Don't worry. It's okay. I've ironed things out with the detective. I think."

"I hope so. Just don't do anything stupid, and if you do, let me know first so I can make sure you are represented by counsel, okay?"

"You know me."

"Yes, I do know you, that's the problem."

"Okay, okay, I got it. Let me continue. So, there were these amenity baskets…"

"Amenity baskets?"

"They're like gift baskets. They filled them with muffins and fruit juice and then dropped them off to each of us on the first night."

"Nice."

"Very, right? The next night we got a mono-grammed cap. But I digress. Anyway, something looks a little off with the flowers in one of the baskets—the one the guy who dropped dead received—and I'm wondering if you could ask Diego to have the forensics lab take a look and let me know what they see."

"Why don't you ask him yourself?"

"It's, well, it's complicated. I haven't really talked to him since I returned to Carmel and the way we left things was a little on the messy side, you know?"

"You mean after your dad's retirement party? Yeah, I get it. Okay, send me the pictures. I'll call Diego and talk to him before forwarding them to the lab and see what I can find out."

"I appreciate that."

"Be smart, Sam."

"I always am."

I mean, right?

CHAPTER THIRTEEN

I spent the day taking a nice long nap and a dip in the ocean (so warm! especially compared to the water in the Monterey Bay), which helped me start to feel human again after my all-nighter. At 5:45 p.m., I started my walk down the stairs at the Mokihana Resort & Spa for what was originally scheduled as the final gathering of the trip. This one was not a reception by the pool or a luau on the beach but dinner on the private patio outside their signature restaurant, the Ma'o Hau Hele (the Hawaiian name for hibiscus, the state flower). Just as I was starting down, my phone buzzed, and a picture of a dachshund-schnauzer-lab mix popped up: Lizzy's dog Canoodle.

"Hello Lizzy," I said, knowing I was about to get it.

"What the heckety heck are you doing out there, Sam?" Lizzy said, the sound of clanking glasses and dogs barking in the background.

"Nice to hear from you, as well," I said, stopping in a small alcove and sitting on a bench next to a huge sculpture that appeared to be a real Botero.

"I haven't heard from *you*, that's for sure," Lizzy said. "I had to hear from Diego who heard from your uncle that you are somehow involved in a murder on your first press trip?"

"It's not a murder, per se, as much as a death that may or may not be suspicious in nature."

"Horse hockey."

"What's horse hockey?"

"You're investigating something. What's going on?" The noise level started to get a little raucous—some particularly yappy dogs having a heated conversation. "Just a second, let me go back into my office..." Things got much quieter. "Okay, shoot."

"Busy day at the Paw's Up?"

"Normal. You should have seen it here yesterday. We hosted an unofficial launch for Carmel's Poodle Day event last night. Terry's Lounge at the Cypress Inn will host them this afternoon after the parade."

"So, today you have every type of dog but poodles?"

"Pretty much. But let's not get off the subject. Tell me what's going on with the dead guy."

"I'm not sure. Really, I'm not sure. He was this strange old dude who wore an ascot…"

"In Hawaii?"

"Yes, thank you! I called him Alistair the Ascot. On the first night at the reception, he told me he had a seasickness patch to help with the boat ride, so I went to his suite."

"Oh, Sam."

"Yeah, yeah. When I heard the Jacuzzi jets start up I skedaddled and then the next morning while I was getting my Lomi-Lomi massage…"

"Well, look at you, la de da."

"I know, right? Anyway, they brought us all in—spa robes and all—and announced that the Ascot had died and that the circumstances were suspicious. And here's this: At first, they thought it involved blunt force cranial trauma, but it ends up his heart stopped."

"So, what's the big deal, then? He had a heart attack and hit his head."

"You would think so, but they think there might have been something in his system that induced the heart attack."

"Induced? Oh. Wow."

"Right? Wow is right. And here's the other thing: Everybody hated the dude."

"Everybody?"

"Everybody! I had just met him, and he was a cad but a manageable cad, you know? I dealt with a lot worse at the paper and over at the court-house. But the other writers had all had some sort of altercation with Alistair over the years and the people in the hotel industry also hated him but needed the coverage he gave them on his radio show so put up with him."

"Okay, that's a lot to take in but go on. Where do things stand now?"

"I'm headed to what was originally scheduled as the final dinner for the trip. I'm assuming they will let us know exactly what they're going to be doing with us and when we will be able to leave."

"Well, they can't let anybody leave until they find out exactly what killed him."

"You said it."

"Wow," Lizzy laughed. "You do manage to find yourself in some situations, my friend—even in the most unlikely of places."

"I know, right?"

"So, what is YOUR plan?"

"Well, Roger…"

"Who's Roger?"

"The detective."

"And you call him Roger? As in Federer?"

"As in the Fed himself."

"That's cool but, well, he lets you call him Roger? Is that a Hawaiian thing?"

"It's more a getting-to-know-each-other-a-bit-better thing."

"Oooo. Nice."

"It's not like that, Lizzy, although he is quite intelligent and has a really nice smile."

"Very nice."

"Yeah, yeah. Anyway, Roger said I should let them do their job, so I'll do that."

"Sure, you will."

"I will. Unless, of course, I happen to find something that might help with the investigation."

"Well, of course."

"Speaking of which, I'd better get going to this dinner and find out how their day went riding bikes down Haleakala. Really bummed I missed that."

"Maybe you can do it tomorrow—especially since it sounds like you're going to be staying awhile."

"That's a good idea. I'll ask."

"All right, I'll let you go then. Be safe, Sam."

"I always am."

"Yeah, right. You forget that I know you."

I stood up, smoothed my skirt, and continued down to our final dinner (or at least, what was originally scheduled as our final dinner). Even after talking with Lizzy, I was only five minutes late, and luckily, as I walked around the outside of the open-air restaurant, everyone looked to still be gathering. Based on Mona's original information and stories told by the others, most press trips had at least one person who was perpetually late (as in at least 20-30 minutes late). This particular group was so ridiculously on time I was starting to worry that I was that person.

I was glad to see them still in cocktail-mode—standing around with their drinks chatting on the patio outside the Ma'o Hau Hele, Mokihana Resort's signature restaurant. When I got to the host desk in the restaurant, I pointed over to the group standing outside and they nodded and I made my way out to meet them.

"Sam!" Brittany was doing her squeaky scream and wave again, which ruined my ability to sneak in unnoticed.

I scanned the crowd to see who all was there. Taylor was standing next to Brandon doing what I assumed was her impression of flirting by flipping her black hair back and lightly putting her hand on his forearm. Interesting. Mac and Frank were still thick as thieves (as they say). They were at the bar and seemed to be trying to decide which local beer they should try if their pointing of fingers was any indication. Ed, Dorothy, and Brian—the "elders" as it were—were standing in a threesome, all smiles as they chatted away.

Brittany continued her gesturing, so I immediately walked over to her. She was standing next to Trevor and, get this, giggling as she looked at the pictures and videos he was showing her on his iPhone. I had never seen this side of her. It must have been some bike ride.

"You should see the amazing shots Trevor got from his GoPro on today's bike ride," said Brittany. And then, realizing that I had not been on it (and why—although I don't know if she knew exactly why I'd spent the night at the jail with Detective Kai), she added, "Oh, I'm so sorry you missed it."

"I am, too."

"I hope you were able to help Detective Kai," said Brittany.

"I hope so, too."

"What did he ask you about?"

"Just what Alistair's room looked like when I was in there that first night to get the seasickness patch." I didn't think they needed to know about my other visit to the room.

"That's it, huh?"

"Yeah, that's it," I said.

"You had to go all the way to the police station to do that?" Trevor asked.

"Yeah. They wanted me to compare what I saw with the pictures they had of what everything looked like when they arrived."

"So, what did you see?" Brittany asked as I noticed the others walking a little closer and leaning into our conversation a bit.

"Nothing out of the ordinary that I could see except, well, the two amenity baskets…" I looked over at Dorothy, who sighed, "…plus a bottle of Veuve Clicquot champagne in a bucket with a card…" Now it was Brittany's turn to sigh. "And the printed itinerary with his notes."

It was hard to miss Brittany and Brandon's questioning looks. "From what I could see, it looked like he loved the resort."

"Well, that's nice to hear at least," said Brandon.

"I don't get it," I heard Taylor say behind me to my left. "So, the old asshole drops dead. Why is that still our problem?"

"I guess it's just not as clear-cut as that," I said.

"What does that mean?" said Fred, to my right.

"I guess they still don't have a clear answer as to how he died."

"Strange," said Dorothy.

There was nodding all around and then a moment as they took it all in. Then Brandon tried to lighten the situation.

"Well, until they do figure out what happened, you all are welcome to continue to stay here at the resort," he said. "As long as you need."

"And, actually," Brittany said, "we have good news. We set up a spa day for everyone tomorrow, since you didn't get to enjoy it when, well, you know…"

"Yes. We were going to announce that at dinner, but since we're all here and talking about it, we thought you would like to know," said Brandon, smiling that million-watt smile of his. Man, he was good-looking. Really just objectively beautiful the same way the Botero statue I had been sitting next to when I talked to Lizzy was. It made me wonder how often he ran into phone booths—if there were any left on the island—and tore off his Clark Kent glasses to go and save hapless tourists from impending doom.

"A spa day sounds wonderful. At least there's something good that Alistair's done," Taylor said, clinking glasses with Dorothy.

"I can't wait to hear about the bike ride," I said, hoping to change the subject a bit. "I'm so sorry I missed it."

"We are, too," said Brandon.

"Since we are staying a little longer, perhaps I can do it another time?"

"I can take you tomorrow morning if you would like," Frank said, piping up. He was holding a Bikini Blond lager from Maui Brewing Company in his hand, which matched the one in Mac's hand. Guess they had made their choice. "Then you can enjoy the spa in the afternoon."

Brandon and Brittany nodded in agreement.

"You would do that?"

"Sure," said Frank.

"That's another early morning for you, Frank. Are you sure you want to do that?"

"Of course. With one person, we don't have to be quite as crazy about the hour. Typically, the companies that specialize in the tours—including the one we used this morning—have to start early because of the different hotel pickups and the time it takes to get everyone up to the top of the crater and set up for the sunrise. They give a little history while up there and then start the ride down once the sun is up and everybody is set up on their bikes. That all takes a while. But since I'll be taking you myself and using the hotel van and bikes—which we do for our VIPs who want a private tour—I can give you the history on the drive up. We can time it to get there just in time for the sunrise and then do the bike ride from the park down through Makawao to Paia like we did today. So, maybe we leave around 5 a.m.?"

"That would be perfect," I said.

153

"Great," Frank said. "Just remember to wear a jacket and long pants—it gets chilly at the top of Haleakala."

"Will do."

Brittany smiled. "Oh, this makes me so happy!"

"Me, too," said Brandon, who then looked over at Chef Marc, who was gesturing toward the table they had set up for us.

"Looks like it's time to eat," Brandon said, then walked with me over to the table. "I'm so glad you're going to get to experience the ride for your story, Sam. If there's anything else you would like to see over on that side of the island, just let Frank know. We won't schedule your spa treatment until late in the afternoon so you will have plenty of time."

"That's so great. Thank you!"

"You are most welcome. We're all just so sorry you got entangled in this mess. I have to admit I'm surprised they're still investigating it. I really thought he must have died of natural causes."

"I guess there is a lot that is still kind of inconclusive."

"Inconclusive? What an odd word to use."

"I know. That's what I thought. But that's what Detective Kai said. Inconclusive—and not just the way he died, but I guess there's something odd about the security tapes they examined from outside Alistair's suite."

"What does that mean?"

"Again, I don't know. It was just something he mentioned."

154

Brandon shook his head and shrugged. "Oh well, I guess there's nothing we can do about it, and if the resort has your lovely presence around for a few more days, so much the better."

He smiled and pointed to the table that had been set immaculately for our dinner. "I can tell you that you're in for a treat tonight."

CHAPTER FOURTEEN

Before I knew it, my alarm was going off. I looked over at my phone and the display read "4:45 a.m." Ugh. Again, I noted to myself that a midday bike ride down Haleakala would have been just as lovely. But this was work, I reminded myself. It was just hard to remember that after a decadent five-course meal that had some pretty amazing wines paired with each course (no, none of them were from the Maui winery—sorry, Maui winery). The dinner also included a lot of laughing among the group. An easy camaraderie had formed after spending three days—not to mention dealing with a lot of unforeseen drama—together.

I slept in the clothes I was going to wear so after I turned off the alarm, I hopped out of bed, brushed my teeth, pulled my hair through the back of my new Mokihana Resort cap, and made my way down to the porte-cochere. It was still dark when I arrived at exactly 5 a.m. (proud of myself!) and found Frank waiting beside a black SUV emblazoned with the Mokihana Resort logo and two bikes attached to the back. Sassy. Even sassier, Simone, the coffee cart gal from Harrisburg, was standing beside him holding a cup of coffee and the exact smoothie (kale, cucumber, apple, and ginger) I had picked up each of the two days before.

"I can't believe you remembered."

"It's the kind of service we like to offer everyone at the Mokihana Resort, Sam," Simone said with a smile.

"I'm impressed."

Fred's comment about how this kind of treatment was a big part of the draw in this line of work came ringing back. It was easy to see how this life of luxury hotels could become addictive.

I thanked Simone, got into the car with Frank, and we headed off. Even in the dark, I could make out that we were taking the same route we had the day we visited the Upcountry farms. We drove past the abandoned sugar cane factory and then turned up the road that led past a number of the farms, this time to take us to the top of Haleakala.

Like the previous trip, Frank was rattling on with his spiel about the history of the area. I have to admit my head was too thick to take in most of it. I was alternating swigs from my coffee and my smoothie hoping it would help my brain wake up when I felt the unmistakable vibration from my phone that meant a text had come in.

I took a look. Diego. It was weird getting a message from him after all this time but since I had asked Uncle Henry to contact him about the flowers in the amenity baskets it was not completely unexpected.

"If you don't mind, Frank, I have to take a look at this," I said to Frank.

"No problem," Frank said, humming away like the chipper guy he always seemed to be.

I looked at the text—a series of texts, it looked like—and it read: "Sorry to send this so early your time, but I wanted to get back to you about those flowers."

"There's one of them that, while tropical looking, is actually *adenium obesum*. It's known as the impala lily, mock azalea, Sabi star, or by its most common name—the desert rose. As its name suggests, the desert rose grows on a semi-succulent shrub or small tree from the *apocynaceae* family. Sorry to give you so much technical information, but I wasn't sure why you needed it."

I scrolled to the next text. "Anyway, the desert rose can have a pretty high toxicity level because of the cardiac glycosides. Ingestion of any part of the plant or even the sap of the plant can cause gastrointestinal pain, diarrhea, vomiting, hyper-salivation, and mouth and throat discomfort, and can be fatal for people with other underlying conditions."

Interesting. The stomach problems Alistair mentioned made sense, then. Add in possible heart issues and it might have been just enough to make his death "inconclusive."

Another text came in: "Also, as I mentioned, it's a little odd to find it in a tropical place like Hawaii. It's more likely to be grown in dry desert climates like those in the Southwest."

I waited a moment. The texts stopped coming so I started crafting my response.

"Thank you, Diego," I texted back. "If you can believe it, I am already up and about this morning. I'm on my way to ride a bike down the side of a volcano." I added a scared smiley face emoji, then pondered for a moment to figure out what else to say before adding an awkward: "Thanks again for your help. When I get home, let's catch up."

I put the phone down. Desert rose. Huh. Who could have brought a plant like that to Hawaii?

"Everything okay?" Frank asked.

"Oh, yeah, fine, just a text from home."

"Where is home for you, Sam?"

"Carmel, California."

"That's right. You mentioned that before."

"And you are from Arizona, according to your tag at least," I said.

"I am. Born and bred. Actually, I lived there until about six months ago."

Just then we reached the guard gate that would let us into Haleakala National Park. Frank leaned out his window and showed the ranger the resort's national park pass. We then continued on up to the visitor center and parked.

I got out of the car and immediately looked up. It was hard not to. While the sky was still dark, there were a million stars. It was like you could touch them. Just gorgeous. I zipped my jacket up because it was also—as Frank had warned—pretty darn cold up at 10,000 feet (42 degrees Fahrenheit, according to my phone).

"Look at the stars," I said.

"Pretty amazing, huh? That's why you want to get here so early in the morning. Soon you'll see the next reason."

We leaned against the van, and true to Frank's word, it wasn't long before the stars started to fade, the sky got lighter, and the sun began to appear over the horizon. We were up above the coastal clouds so once the sun emerged through them it illuminated the peaks surrounding the Haleakala crater. The red and rust colors of the crater began to blend with the grays and blues of the clouds and the golden orange orb in the distance. It was just spectacular. I caught as many moments as I could with my iPhone but also made a mental note to ask Dorothy if I could see her photos. I'm sure she got some amazing shots with her Nikon.

"This is just gorgeous."

"Isn't it?" Frank said. "One of the reasons I was not unhappy to come up again with you today, Sam. You can really never see it too many times."

"Spectacular."

"Of course, one of the secrets is that it's just as gorgeous at sunset—and then you can stargaze after the sun goes down."

"I knew it! I knew we didn't have to get up at this ungodly hour."

Frank laughed. "You really don't—although you can't really ride a bike down the road once the sun has gone down. This way we have the rest of the morning to catch the views on the way down."

"I was going to ask you about that."

"About what?"

"Our ride down. What route are we taking?"

"Most people ride down the park road through Hula and then when you hit Makawao head over to either Haiku or Paia. Yesterday, we went to Paia."

"What if I was looking for something a little off the beaten path?"

"Meaning?"

"My editor is keen on finding something special. She said *Travel & Leisure* wrote about a trail through a eucalyptus grove near Kula."

"Oh, yeah, that's cool. We could do that."

"Is there maybe something else? Something special we could add on?"

"There is a path that Elua told me about."

"Elua?"

"He's one of our bellmen—I think he greeted you at the airport."

"Oh, the Hawaiian hunk," I said. "Sorry, that was my nickname for him."

161

Frank laughed. "Yeah, I guess he is quite the looker. Anyway, he's from Hana, which is on the other side of the crater, as the crow flies, so he knows these places like the back of his hand."

"And?"

"And, well, a lot of these paths they don't want people to know or write about."

"Which I totally get. You don't want tons of tourists trampling gorgeous local places just to get a picture for Instagram."

"Yeah, they kind of frown on that." Frank's face got a sad Charlie Brown look that almost made me laugh out loud it was so cute.

"Totally understandable. Again, I totally get that and have no desire to ruin any local treasures."

"There is this one path Elua showed me on one of our days off. It starts between Makawao and Paia and runs alongside a zipline course that was put in a few years ago over one of the canals that takes water from the mountain down to the sea. It has views of some pretty spectacular waterfalls and streams and then drops you off on the Hana Highway not too far from Mama's Fish House at the beach. You know Mama's, right? It's an island institution, and you should definitely see it even if we don't get to eat there."

"That sounds perfect. I have heard of Mama's, so it would be great to see it for myself to mention in the story."

"This path is not that well known, but since the zip line is already there, and it's not on any land the locals consider sacred, Elua said they don't care if people know or write about it. He specifically showed it to me as something to offer the guests who want something a little off the beaten path. I confirmed it all with Clive as well. They both said that by sending people on this trail, it might keep them off those where the locals really don't want any tourists."

"That sounds absolutely perfect for the readers of *Carmel Today* magazine. We can give them a little adventure and then suggest a nice cocktail and freshly caught Mahi Mahi at Mama's Fish House to top it off."

"Great. Let's do that, then," said Frank. "I will radio Elua back at the bell desk and let him know to have someone pick the SUV up here and meet us down at Mama's instead of Paia at noon."

"I love it. Again, it sounds just perfect. Thank you, Frank."

Frank radioed back to the hotel. Then we got our bikes off the back of the SUV, put our helmets on, and were off. The ride down was a total blast—flying down thousands of feet through 20-plus switchbacks. I have to say, for someone who didn't grow up here, Frank hit the switchbacks like a champ. I had to slow down a few times myself as I rounded the turns—keeping in mind the advice he gave me just before we took off not to brake too hard when I hit the turns as that would throw me off the bike. No, thank you!

When the switchbacks ended, we merged onto Haleakala Highway, where things straightened out a bit. As we got into the town of Kula, I saw signs with directions pointing to a number of the farms we had visited earlier. Good times.

At a pull-out right after the Kula Lodge Restaurant that had some benches, Frank pulled over to let me catch up—and catch my breath, which was much needed. As we stopped, I could feel my phone buzzing away in my pocket but ignored it. Whoever it was could wait.

"It's a blast, huh?" Frank asked.

"Oh my god, so fun! I'm so happy I got to do this, especially after not getting much exercise the last few days—beyond trooping on and off the van, of course."

"Do you need some water?"

"That would be great."

While Frank pulled the water bottles out of his pack, I did a quick check of the text messages. One—well, actually, six it appeared—was from Brittany.

"Here you go," Frank said, handing me the water before I had a chance to look to see what they said.

"Thank you." I took a much-needed swig. "I have to say, you were amazing on those corners."

"I was a big mountain biker growing up in Arizona."

"That's right, you're from Tempe. That's in the Phoenix area, right?" He nodded. "What brought you out here?"

"The job. I was let go from the job I had right after college at Arizona State."

"Not a bad job to fall into."

"Right? It's pretty rad."

I smiled at his use of the same word as Mac. "Where did you work in Phoenix? Another hotel?"

"No, this is my first."

"You're going to be spoiled."

"Totally spoiled! It's such a wonderful place. I was so happy when they opened the activity center and asked me to help out."

"It really is wonderful," I said—and I meant it. "What did you do before?"

"Kind of similar. I was the activities director at an assisted living facility."

"That must have been tough," I said. "My dad is in one now—memory care."

"Oh, that's rough. I'm sorry. But I actually loved it. If you haven't guessed, I'm a big people person and our residents had so many amazing stories."

"You're a good kid, Frank."

"Thanks!" He pointed down the hill toward Makawao, our next stop. "Shall we? We can stop in Makawao for a bite to eat. The hotel packed us a nice little snack box."

"They really go all out, don't they?"

"You should see the customer service training they give us."

"I can only imagine."

"Yeah, it's pretty extensive, but it really helps us think through everything that the guests might need so we can always be looking to add a little something extra."

"Like Simone remembering my smoothie every morning."

"Exactly. As you've learned, those touches go a long way with people. And the Mokihana Resort treats us just as well. Ms. Chang says the hotel's motto—something they do in all the best hotels— is that 'If the back of the house is happy, the front of the house is happy.' I can tell you honestly that this back of the house is very happy."

Frank gave such a big smile I really had to hold back from pinching his little cheeks.

"After we have our stop in Makawao," he continued, seemingly thinking it all through on the spot, "I'll show you the path that goes by the canal in the jungle used by the zip line folks. Like I said, it goes right by this really cool waterfall before heading down toward the ocean and coming out on Holomua Road. That's the street Mama's Fish House is on and also near Ho'okipa, where all the kite surfers hang out."

"It sounds wonderful. Lead the way."

CHAPTER FIFTEEN

We continued riding down Haleakala Highway. After passing a polo arena, we rode by a high school and a performing arts center. We then made a right onto Kula Highway and then a slight right to merge onto Makawao Avenue, which Frank said would take us into the town of Makawao.

As an indication we were getting close, I saw a sign saying "Aloha from Historic Makawao. Paniolo Country." More with the cowboys—or, as I learned the other day—paniolos. When we reached Baldwin Avenue, the main part of the town emerged with its colorful wooden buildings. It was the second time in a week I felt like I'd been transported back to an old Western. Frank, of course, dutifully let me know that the buildings were indeed leftover from the town's early days as the center of the paniolo culture. We got off and walked our bikes. I noted that while the vibe of the building exteriors was 1900s ranch life, closer inspection revealed interiors filled with fine art galleries, glass-blowing demonstrations, jewelry and trinket shops, yoga studios, and other wellness-related entities.

In other words, by the time Frank informed me that—while the area did still have a number of ranches, the town itself had become more of an art-and-wellness community—I had pretty much already figured it out. We stopped at a small park with a sign saying "Da Market" hanging on the fence. Inside, the park was filled with produce and craft vendors sitting behind temporary tables while a singer played Hawaiian songs on the guitar. Okay, now I was back in Hawaii.

"Want to grab a quick bite?" Frank asked.

"That sounds great. The smoothie kind of wore off."

We found a picnic table and Frank pulled out some resort-prepared granola and yogurt—which looked amazing after riding 18 miles down the side of a volcano. He then added some fruit drinks, which reminded me of the flower in the amenity basket.

"Have you ever heard of a desert rose, Frank?"

"Sure, who hasn't?"

Lots of people, I would think, but instead, I said: "Have you heard of it being grown around here?"

"No, well, at least not on most of the Hawaiian Islands, which have a more humid environment than the desert rose likes. Of course, there are parts of the Big Island—which has a larger variety of climates than the others—where you might be able to grow it. But I don't think it's a native species. Really, I think it needs to be grown in a traditional Southwestern desert climate—like the one where I'm from in Tempe."

"Wow. You know a LOT about them."

"Oh, yeah. We had them growing all over our backyard when I was growing up. My Mom was constantly reminding me not to let our dog eat them as they can be poisonous."

Frank said this with no guile at all, which made it hard to believe he might have been guilty of trying to poison Alistair. Besides, what in the world would his motive possibly be?

"So I heard," I said before realizing I had forgotten to look at my phone to see the texts from Brittany.

"Do you mind?" I asked, holding up my phone.

"Not at all. Just enjoying the moment," Frank said, smiling and giving the Hawaiian shaka sign to the guy playing the guitar, who smiled and nodded in return. Clive and Elua's tutelage was obviously rubbing off on the boy.

I took a quick look at my phone. Amid the jumble of emojis and exclamation points, the texts from Brittany seemed to have something to do with Frank and the security tapes and him lying on his application. I looked over at Frank, and he smiled back with that big goofy grin of his and gave me a thumbs up. It still just didn't make sense, but I didn't want him to see the message, so I smiled back and put the phone down. I figured I could look more closely at what Brittany was saying when we got down to Mama's Fish House and were picked up by Elua.

"Anything important?" Frank asked.

"Just a note from Brittany letting me know my spa treatment is at 3 o'clock."

Frank looked at his watch. "It's 10:30 now, so we should have plenty of time, but whenever you're ready, we can continue down."

"I'll let Brittany know."

"Sounds good." Frank started packing up the drink and snack fixings while I sent a quick text to Brittany. I told her we would be heading down a trail that would drop us near Mama's Fish House and that Frank had radioed to have us picked up there by someone on the bell staff. Then, just to allay her fears, I told her that if she wanted to track us, I would add her to the "find your phone" app on my iPhone and then did just that. I figured it wouldn't hurt to have someone know where we were going to be. While I still didn't think Frank could have killed Alistair, he did say he had only done this path once before with Elua and I didn't want us getting lost without anyone tracking us.

We walked our bikes back out to Baldwin Avenue, got back on, and started heading down. As we passed the edge of the town of Makawao, Frank called back to tell me that if we followed the street all the way to the ocean it would take us into the town of Paia, which is the ride they had done the day before. I could see the ocean in the distance as we continued down the winding road. We passed signs indicating an art center, the entrance to a wellness retreat, and other structures I could see but not really identify, along with houses that ranged from sumptuous to shacks — sometimes right next to each other.

Frank signaled to me that we would be turning right onto a small road that went perpendicular to the ocean for a while. When we curved back down the hill, things suddenly got a lot more rural and jungle filled. We even passed a small grove of pine trees that smelled like the ones back in Carmel. Soon, we saw a large gulch running along the right side of the path. It only had a little water in it, but I was guessing it could get quite flooded during big storms. Big white poles had red paint over a good three feet of the bottom portion. Next to them were signs indicating not to try to drive through if you couldn't see the red portion.

Frank pointed to the other side of the gulch and said that was where a private property owner had allowed a local company to build a zip line. Soon, we turned to our right again and crossed over the gulch via a rather sketchy (in my opinion) bridge onto that property. After we crossed to the other side of the bridge, we turned back down a path that now placed the gulch on our left side. I could again see the ocean far in the distance ahead. When I looked up to peek above the trees, I noticed the zip line cables high above. Every once in a while, bodies would come flying down the hill above us screaming in delight or terror—it was actually hard to tell the difference.

As we continued down, we entered an area that was really thick with trees and bushes and vines. I lost sight of the ocean and, although I could still hear the screams, couldn't even see the zip line cables above us. There was just enough room for our bikes to get through, so we rode much more slowly than we had before.

As Frank had promised, we passed a gorgeous view of a waterfall that fed into a stream and then into this part of the gulch. I'm sure it offered beautiful views for the screaming people up on the zip line. I was just thinking about how I would describe this part of our bike ride in the story—with a disclaimer that only the most intrepid of *Carmel Today* readers should give it a try—when I saw a clearing ahead. It was filled with a lot of sunlight, and I was happy to see the riding should start to get a little easier for us.

"We're about to enter private property not used by the zip line," Frank shouted back. "But don't worry. Elua said the owners are cool with people traveling through."

When he hit the sunlight, Frank looked back and smiled and gave a thumbs up. Just then a shot rang out and I saw him fly off his bike.

Maybe the owners weren't so cool about it after all.

CHAPTER SIXTEEN

I couldn't believe what I'd just seen. Where did Frank go? And what was that shot? As I careened out of the jungle into the clearing where Frank went down and pulled the brakes on my bike, I saw him—and it wasn't some irate landowner holding a shotgun.

Then it came back to me—just what it was in the picture in the newspaper clipping in Alistair's room that had triggered something in my brain, just what it was in the blurry image that looked so familiar: those goddamn teeth of his.

"I'm going to need you to stop right there," Brandon said, holding a handgun on me.

I slowly got off my bike to show him I wasn't going to do anything stupid (yet—truth be told I wasn't exactly sure what I was going to do). I let my bike fall to the ground and held my hands up in the air where he could see them.

"I was hoping I was wrong," I said as calmly as I could even though my heart was pounding through my chest. I used my peripheral vision to try to look around for Frank. To the right, I saw the divot marks from where his bike had gone into a sugar cane field. There was no other movement. To my left was a road and one of the Mokihana Resort SUVs, which I am guessing was how Brandon came to find us.

"Wrong?" Brandon asked.

"That it was you in the picture."

"Picture?"

"The one in Alistair's room on the article about the botched hotel opening in Scottsdale—even if they didn't identify you by name."

"Smart girl," Brandon said. To his credit, he actually looked a little sad as he did.

"But why kill Alistair?"

"I didn't want to. When I saw his name on the press trip list, I originally just wanted to make him sick enough that he'd stay in his room—sorry, his fucking suite—during the trip."

"You were hoping he wouldn't recognize you."

"It has been more than a decade since he wrote that story, and although he attended the opening of that hotel, I never spent all that much time with him. I was actually hoping that by now he would have forgotten my name and face."

"So, you used the desert rose…"

Brandon looked impressed as he raised his eyebrows and nodded. "Again, smart girl. Yes. The resort has a florist that grows it in a greenhouse for us to use in the arrangements. It is a gorgeous flower—it just shouldn't be put right next to muffins or, more accurately, have any of the sap that flows through its roots, stems, leaves, and bark rubbed on those muffins or dipped in the fruit juice."

That was startlingly specific. "Sounds like you've used it before."

"I have had some experience with the plant, yes. And, before you even think about doing something stupid, I have also had some experience with guns."

I realized there was something that didn't add up: "So, wait, I'm confused, why did you go back, then, and hit Alistair on the head?"

Brandon paused for a moment as if wondering if he should bother to answer and then looked at his gun, shrugged, and said: "When he left the reception early, I wondered what happened. Then I saw you leaving his room—again, I apologize, his *suite,* and knew I had an opening to see just how much he remembered."

The venom that spewed out of his mouth when he said the word "suite" reminded me, in a funny way, of how Alistair had been able to change his countenance on a dime, as well. Suddenly gone was the benevolent sales director with the amazing smile. "Naturally, he was a bit of an ass when he saw me, and well, I guess I lost control."

"What could he have possibly said to make you want to kill him?"

"Alistair told me he recognized my name from the itinerary Brittany emailed him. He actually pulled up and printed that review he had written all those years ago. Can you believe that? When I confronted him, he said he wasn't sure he was right until after he saw me at the reception and that obviously I was the same idiot I had been then."

"What was in that story that was so bad? What could possibly be that important?"

Brandon thought for a moment. "Only everything I had worked for." On my confused look, he sighed and continued. "If you must know, I had been given the chance to open my first luxury hotel as a general manager—it was a Relais & Chateaux–level hotel, Sam."

The words meant nothing to me, but I nodded as if they did, and he continued: "It was a beautiful boutique hotel in Scottsdale. Just exquisite. I oversaw the designers, hired all the personnel, and was going to run it. It was going to be wonderful. I even moved my mother into an assisted living facility nearby in Phoenix as I thought I was going to be there for a very long time.

"Then the economy tanked, and the ownership group lost all their funding three months before we opened the doors. I begged them to hold off on the opening until we could make sure everything was perfect. So much still needed to be done. But they wouldn't listen—they wanted the revenue that guests would bring—and made me hold a big grand opening and invite journalists. It was a fucking nightmare, Sam. So much of the hotel just wasn't finished, and the elements that would take it to the luxury level were lacking. Alistair's review in *USA Today*—fucking *USA Today*, Sam—made it sound like it was all my fault. I was black-balled in the industry, at least at the luxury level, and had to start all over again."

Brandon was so angry he began pacing. "I had been working for the likes of Four Seasons and Ritz-Carltons. I was going to be one of the youngest general managers of a luxury property in the world. But after that botched opening—which was the owners' fault and Alistair knew it… HE KNEW IT when he wrote that review, and he still threw me under the bus—I had to go work as a group sales manager for a Marriott. A Marriott. In St. Kitts."

He was really worked up now and said the words with such disdain it was clear that it was quite the sore point. I have to admit I really didn't understand the distinction. I mean, Marriotts seemed like pretty nice hotels to me—of course, for me, if a room has a comfortable bed and good water pressure, I'm a pretty happy camper. Just because someone isn't standing by your van at 5:30 in the morning with your favorite smoothie and the toilet seat in your bathroom isn't heated doesn't mean it isn't a good hotel.…

And, yes, I was a little disturbed that these were the thoughts running through my head while Brandon held a gun on me and continued his lunatic screed about having to work for a Marriott in the Caribbean before working his way back into luxury hotel management—and even then, as he pointed out, as director of sales and not general manger.

Then it occurred to me, and perhaps I shouldn't have said this out loud to a man holding a gun on me, but I did: "You do realize that they never would have looked into his death without that cranial injury," I said.

"Come again?"

"The bump on his head is not what killed him," I said, figuring that at the very least I could buy some time until I could figure out what to do. "With his terrible state of health, the toxins in the desert rose stopped his heart. No one ever would have looked into his death without the bump on the head. And, even if they did figure out it was a toxic flower, it would be hard to pin that on anybody."

"So?"

"So, you totally could have gotten away with it. Today, all of us would have been flying home after a wonderful press trip—albeit somewhat sad because of Alistair's untimely death—and no one would have been the wiser."

"Oh, Sam, I'm still going to get away with it," Brandon said, his million-dollar smile becoming even more malevolent.

"But... you just shot Frank..."

"Yes, poor boy. Did you know I helped him get this job? He was really good to my mother after her stroke. Then he lost that job after being labeled as negligent in her death."

"Desert rose again?"

"As you've noted, it's an effective plant for those with compromised immune systems. After the stroke, hers was very compromised. It was her time, really."

Wow, sociopath much? "So, why did you help him get the job at the Mokihana?"

"Well, he took the fall for me, didn't he? I didn't mean for that to happen, but they found the flowers nearby and assumed he had been negligent in putting them so close to her food."

Now I was even more confused. "Then why shoot him now?"

"Because now I can pin this on the two of you..." Brandon said. "You yourself told me the cops weren't letting this go and were looking into the changes I made to the security tapes. So, I also altered Frank's employment documents. Now I can set it up to look like he was a spurned lover involved in the death of the lecherous old man who hit on you before killing you himself."

"That's ridiculous..."

"Is it? Everyone knew that Alistair was a cad..."

Before I could tell him that I was pretty sure Frank was gay, I heard some rustling in the fields and saw Frank starting to sit up. He looked very disoriented and had a big red splotch running down his shoulder. Brandon turned to look as well, and I saw my chance for escape. Banking on the fact that Brandon probably wasn't all that well versed in shooting, I quickly ducked down and ran back into the jungle, which was only about 30 feet behind me. I heard a shot ricochet off one of the trees right above me so decided to ignore the path and instead ran straight into the thickest part of the vegetation, using the fact I was smaller and lighter than Brandon to my advantage as I crouched my way through the jungle. I tried to protect my face with my arms but was still getting quite the thrashing from the branches.

I kept heading uphill, away from the ocean. At a certain point, I stopped and scooched even farther down under a thicket of branches with abundant leaves. I listened to see if I could hear how far back behind me Brandon might be. I didn't hear a lot of thrashing as much as some faraway footsteps so I was thinking he might have stayed on the path, although the sound of the screaming zip liners above me made it hard to actually tell.

As I looked in the opposite direction from where I'd come from, I noticed a little more light coming through part of the foliage. I tiptoed as quickly as I could until I came to a small clearing. There, I came upon an unexpected sight: a tall thin older man holding some serious pruning shears. He had a long white beard and white hair pulled back in a ponytail and was tending to what may or may not have been a legal (at least in some states) plot of agriculture.

CHAPTER
SEVENTEEN

The man with the shears looked as shocked to see me as I was to see him. I realized I was probably quite the sight. Not only was I thrashed after running through the jungle, but I was also sweating from the heat and humidity, and the curls on my head were making a break to frizz-town under my bike helmet (which I now realized I was still wearing). I snapped the helmet off, held my finger up to my mouth, and whispered, "I'm being chased by a man with a gun," as I pointed back in the general direction of where I had last seen and heard Brandon.

The man nodded without batting an eye—like somehow this wasn't the first time someone had come tearing through the jungle while he was tending to his marijuana crop to say they were being chased by a man with a gun. Not sure how

I felt about that, but by this point, I was too far gone to worry about it.

"My house is not far from here," he whispered. "Come with me."

Weighing the options of following a crazy old man carrying pruning shears versus finding another way to lose Brandon, I decided the man with the shears won out. I noted he was wearing a t-shirt and shorts splotched with paint, so I immediately started calling him (in my head) the Painter. The Painter crossed to the side of the clearing away from where I had come running through the jungle. Initially, it looked like there was nothing but more jungle, but then I noticed a series of walking paths cut into the forest. We took one of the paths and soon reached a fork where one path went up to the right and out to what looked like a huge house or maybe even a compound of houses. It looked vaguely familiar, but before I could figure out where I'd seen it, he pointed at that path, and we started walking in that direction.

Just as we were about to leave the forest and walk onto a series of stepping stones leading to the largest of the buildings on the property, I saw a black SUV heading up the road to the house from the other side. I grabbed the arm of my new pruning-shear-wielding friend—sorry, the Painter—and pointed. We pulled back behind a tree so as not to be seen.

The van slowed as it reached the house and did a slow cruise around the driveway. I could see Brandon in the driver's seat scanning the forest where we were hiding. The Painter nodded, and we slowly and quietly started walking back to the fork in the road and headed in the other direction.

"How did he find us?" I asked and then it dawned on me that it was the same reason he knew where Frank and I were headed on the bike ride: He must have been with Brittany when I gave her the tracking information for my phone.

I held up my phone for the Painter to see.

"He's tracking the phone," I said.

"Turn it off," he said.

"I am. I am."

I turned the phone off, then noticed the path we were on opening up a bit. In the distance, I could see a splotch of red and realized where we were—and why the Painter's compound looked so familiar—we were back on the horseback riding path we had taken out of Kapena Ranch.

"Wait a minute—is that Kapena Ranch?" I pointed at the red splotch that I assumed was the barn in the distance.

"We're actually on ranch property now."

"Your house is on ranch property?"

"It's my ranch."

"I thought it was Kealani's ranch."

"It is. I'm Kealani's father. Grant."

"Nice to meet you, Grant."

"Kealani doesn't need me to run things, so I kind of do my own thing."

"I noticed that." I nodded to the shears.

"Oh, yeah, forgot I had these. Sorry about that. I was taking a break from my painting to, well, you know…"

"I know. Your secret is safe with me. And besides, the shears might come in handy."

"Against a gun, they're not going to help us much."

"True. We need reinforcements."

"That we do." He thought for a minute. "Luckily, they shouldn't be too far from here. The paniolos were scheduled to move the cattle up to graze in the pasture here on the mauka side this morning."

Luckily, I remembered that mauka meant mountain and knew what he meant.

We continued up the riding path we had used two days earlier. When we got close, Grant put his thumb and index finger in his mouth and gave a serious whistle. I had always wanted to learn how to do that but realized this probably wasn't the time to learn.

He whistled again. Soon a lone paniolo on horseback came over the ridge and looked out to see where the sound was coming from. Grant whistled again, and I could see the paniolo spot us. He nodded as he continued down the hill and followed the path into the trees. Before I could process the fact that with his build and frisbee-sized belt buckle he could only be one person, Grant said: "Kekoa, we've got a guy with a gun following us."

"Sam, what are you doing here?" Kekoa asked.

"Being chased by a murderer."

Like Grant, Kekoa took the information in stride and responded with a nod. Really, I don't think anything could rattle the man. I suppose riding 1,000-plus-pound bulls on a regular basis—for fun—could do that to a person.

"We figured out that he was tracking my phone, but we turned it off," I added.

"That bought us a little time but not much," Grant said. "He knows Sam is still in the area, and the ranch is the only property around, so it's not going to take him too long to find her."

"He's also in a car and we're on foot," I added.

"That can be a plus and a minus," Kekoa said. "He can get certain places faster, but there is a lot of terrain on the ranch that's only accessible by horse or foot or mountain bike or maybe an ATV. Speaking of which..." Kekoa pulled out a walkie-talkie. "Loma, can you bring the ATV for Grant? We're in the grove near his stash."

I smiled at the fact that Grant's secret agricultural plot wasn't all that secret.

"I suppose there's a chance he's put my bike in the van so he might have that, too. Not sure if that makes a difference in trying to evade him."

Grant nodded. "We need to bring him to us, but first we need to figure out a way to control his route," said Grant.

"And then be ready when he does," Kekoa said.

"What are you suggesting?"

"We pull him into a place where we can control the environment," said Kekoa.

"I get it," I said. "We set a trap, and then I turn my phone back on and let him track it."

"Exactly," said Grant.

"Makes sense. Do you know where a good place might be?"

"I do," said Grant.

"The feeding station?" Kekoa asked.

Grant nodded at Kekoa, who obviously was on the same Kapena Ranch wavelength and knew exactly what he was talking about.

"That works. We just need to get the crew in place and then bring him there," said Kekoa.

"I can bring him to you," I said.

"Are you sure? We can just take your phone and let him track us."

I couldn't believe I was saying this, but I did. "I don't think it will work unless he sees me with the phone and thinks he has me beat. He doesn't know I met Grant or you, Kekoa, so if he finds me alone, we will have the element of surprise on our side. Besides, I've brought enough trouble on all of you."

Before they could protest, I added, "This is something I need to do."

Grant and Kekoa looked at each other and then nodded. "Okay, we'll play it your way," said Grant.

"That gives me an idea on how this can play out to our maximum advantage and put you in as little danger as possible," said Kekoa. Turning to me, he continued: "Come on, I'll take you and

Grant to the rest of the crew, and then we will get you to your horse."

"I'm sorry—my what?"

CHAPTER EIGHTEEN

"Noe knows what she's doing, Sam." Kekoa's words came back to me as I found myself sitting back on top of Noe, the beautiful dappled gray horse I had ridden—albeit shakily—two days earlier. Kekoa brought her over to me when we reached the group on the upper pasture where the cattle were grazing and reintroduced us. I was polite and asked Noe if she remembered me and gave her a few pets before swinging my legs up and over the saddle. Then the two of us (Noe and me) hid behind a tree on the ridge above the pasture while Grant, Kekoa, and the other paniolos rode off on horses and ATVs toward the red barn and the tail end of the trail we had ridden two days earlier.

Through their binoculars, they had spotted Brandon driving back and forth along the road near Grant's house, so they knew he was a good 15-minute drive from my current location (if he could even find the road) and that he couldn't see where they were going once they left the ridge. Once the paniolos got to the other side of the barn and started up the trail, I pulled my phone out and turned it back on. I sent a quick text to Brittany telling her I was at the Kapena Ranch and to get Detective Kai and meet me here as quickly as possible. Then Noe and I started walking slowly out along the ridge so Brandon could track my steps.

"Okay, Noe, don't let me down," I said, as we started off. I swear she bopped her head up and down in a nod—and this time not because I was holding on to the reins too tight. No, I did as I learned and let her lead the way slowly back toward the barn area, as planned.

From my spot on the ridge, I could see the black SUV Brandon was driving turn around in the driveway at Grant's house and head back down toward the main road that would ultimately take him over to the entrance to Kapena Ranch. At least, that's what I was assuming he was doing and not, you know, deciding to go turn himself in. Wouldn't that be nice? It was a thought that helped me ward off the extreme fear I felt about the plan we had set up, which was going to require me doing a lot of things outside of my comfort zone—and on a horse, no less. I couldn't believe this was my own stupid idea.

Noe and I continued our walk toward the barn area. As I got behind the barn, I saw the black Mokihana Resort SUV start to head up the long road into the ranch. I turned Noe up the hill toward the trail as the SUV skidded to a stop on the other side of the barn. When Brandon jumped out of the car, he looked down at his phone to check the pings for my location. As soon as I saw him do that, I (as instructed) gave Noe a little tap with my heel, raised the reins up loose and high, and said: "Let's go, girl."

That little tap was all I needed for Noe to get the picture and start running up the hill and back into the forested part of the trail we had done two days before. Out of the side of my eye, I saw Brandon look up in surprise as I held on for dear life. Actually, once I got over the shock of flying through the air on top of a horse, I was surprised by how comfortable I felt. Noe was loping or cantering—or whatever they called the flat-out dash she was doing—but I was able to let go and actually enjoy the ride. Okay, so it might have been more enjoyable if I didn't have a crazed sociopath with a gun down the hill behind me, but the point is, I wasn't afraid. I finally understood that thing people talk about when a person and a horse are in sync. It was kind of magical. Or, again, would have been magical if the crazed sociopath wasn't running after us.

As planned, Noe and I continued up the path. I heard the steps far behind me that meant Brandon was running after me. Soon, there was the clearing I was looking for. In the center was a structure filled with hay and other supplies I'm assuming the paniolos needed when moving cattle.

I flew into the clearing and, once I reached the feeding station, pulled off behind it. Kekoa nodded and pulled a shotgun from his pack. He threw it to Grant, who was sitting on the ATV, while the rest of the paniolo all took guns out of their holsters and stood in a line on their horses. I swear I felt like I was in a scene right out of "The Magnificent Seven" when, a few minutes later, a beat-up looking Brandon came thrashing up from the trail to find Grant, Kekoa, and half a dozen other paniolos all holding their shotguns on him.

Brandon's look of surprise quickly faded, and with a shrug, he dropped his gun and put his hands up. A few of the paniolos rode over and used their ropes to tie his hands behind his back.

Just then my phone rang. Brittany. I clicked to accept.

"Sam? Sam? Are you okay? Where ARE you? Detective Kai and I have been following the pings on your phone, but it doesn't look like there's a road into where you are now."

"I'm fine. I'm on the trail above Kapena Ranch. We have Brandon. But you should really first check on Frank," I said. "He was shot in the clearing over by the zip line."

"We already found Frank based on your previous pings. He was just nicked in the shoulder. We bandaged him up, and he should be fine until the medical personnel can get to him. Elua is there and will stay with him, so I joined Detective

Kai when we got your last text. But how can we get to you?"

"Just come back to the barn at the Kapena Ranch. We will come down to meet you."

I nodded at Kekoa, and he smiled and nodded back as he and the other paniolos put Brandon on the back of the ATV and started driving it down to the barn.

I heard Brittany talking to someone. When she came back, she said: "Okay, Detective Kai knows how to get there. We'll be there shortly."

True to her word, it wasn't long before a raft of police cruisers could be seen following Detective Kai's Honda Pilot—which I noted now had the light blaring on top—coming up through the Kapena Ranch gates in the distance. Kealani came out of the barn to greet them as a couple of the paniolos walked Brandon over to the squad cars. Once the ATV was free, Grant jumped on and immediately started heading back up the path to his compound. As I passed him on Noe, he gave me a little smile and a salute, and I returned the gesture.

"Thank you," I said—and really really meant it.

"It was a pleasure," Grant said.

I continued riding Noe down into the crowd of cops and paniolos outside the barn. Detective Kai—Roger—was with them. He turned and smiled when he saw me on Noe. Before I could say anything, Brittany came running out of his car.

"Sam! Sam! Are you alright?"

I jumped off Noe and handed my reins to Kekoa.

"I'm fine," I said, gesturing to her to wait a minute while I finished with Kekoa.

"I can't thank you enough, Kekoa," I said.

"You know, you and Noe looked pretty good out there."

"As you said: Noe knows what she's doing."

"So do you, Sam. So do you."

"Maybe I could take her home with me? She'd be happy in Carmel, right?" A quick mental picture popped up in my head of me and Noe walking up Ocean Avenue and over to Lizzy's cafe to visit with all the pooches.

"I think she will be happier here, but you are welcome to visit her any time."

I gave Noe an extra pet—okay, I gave her a big hug—and then handed the reins to Kekoa.

"Mahalo, Kekoa."

"A'ole pilikia, Sam."

He gave me a smile and the shaka sign and took Noe over to the stables as the other pani-cles started heading back up to the back pasture where I had found them.

I turned back to find Kealani overseeing the bevy of police officers with a grace I could only aspire to someday. As I watched one of them handcuff a by now very scraggly looking Brandon, I was suddenly pulled into the most humongous hug in history by Brittany.

"Oh my god, are you alright? I was so worried—and obviously not just about the *Carmel Today* coverage—ha, listen to me. I'm awful. So, what the hell happened? And was that Grant Willoughby over by the trees? You know he's one of the most famous artists on the island, right? We have his paintings at the hotel and, oh my god, Sam, you had me so so worried."

Brittany continued babbling on and holding me for dear life as I looked over and saw Detective Kai—Roger—standing just beyond. He mouthed, "You okay?" I nodded and we exchanged another smile before he walked over to help the officers put Brandon into one of the police cars—with no sign of those famous teeth to be seen.

CHAPTER NINETEEN

Here's the thing about getting a massage right after you've ridden more than 20 miles on a bicycle, run through a deep thicket of trees, ridden a horse (fast, even!) and, oh yeah, been shot at—it feels really really REALLY good. After giving my statement to the police, I managed to make it back to the hotel in time for my spa appointment. I soon found myself back in a thatched hut above a secluded cove looking down through the massage table at the plumeria they had so thoughtfully placed below. With the sound of the waves hitting the shore, the light breezes blowing through the curtains, and the aromatherapy oils Bettina was using, I pretty much passed out the second she touched my back. I might even have drooled.

After the massage and another dip in the oh-so-soothing ocean, I was refreshed enough to join the rest of the press group for our final Aloha (which, as I'm sure you all know, means both hello and goodbye) dinner. In this case it finally—we hoped, as lovely as the resort was— meant goodbye. Tonight's gathering would be a casual dinner and drinks on the patio outside the resort's lounge, located right off the open-air lobby. As I entered the lounge, I noticed for the first time that one of Grant Willoughby's water-colors—a gorgeous vista with a lone paniolo looking out over the sea on a dappled-gray horse ("Hello, Noe," I said as I looked at the painting)— was prominently displayed over the bar.

"You can't afford it," a voice whispered, and I turned to find Fred entering behind me. He was still wearing his tweed jacket but had added what looked to be a brand new Hawaiian shirt underneath.

"That is a very true statement, Fred. But we can still enjoy it."

"That we can, especially as it looks like there is quite the story behind both that picture and your adventure today. Can't wait to hear it, Nancy Drew."

I smiled. "It was Professor Plum in the study with the candlestick, remember?"

I linked my arm through Fred's, and we walked through the lounge and out onto the patio. A table was set up for the group of us that looked out toward the ocean and had a gorgeous view of the sun as it was just beginning to set. Brittany was already there waiting for us, still clicking through her phone but with a much brighter smile than I'd seen on her face since the day she picked me up at the airport. Fred and I took a couple of seats and were soon joined by Dorothy, Brian, Mac, Taylor, and Trevor.

"Is this everybody?" Brian asked.

"The general manager, Philippa Chang, said she would be stopping by to say hello, but we can go ahead and order drinks while we watch the sunset," said Brittany.

We each ordered one of their signature cocktails. Mine had about 12 ingredients, including a lot of bitters and herbs and things I had never heard of. At its heart, it was a sparkling wine, grapefruit, and Campari concoction that mirrored the colors in the setting sun. Yes, I made sure to take a picture, both of the ingredients in the cocktail and the cocktail itself with the sun setting behind it, to post later on the *Carmel Today* site. I was still technically on duty, after all.

Once the drinks arrived, we all moved or turned or rearranged our chairs in whatever way would allow us to get the best view of the ocean and the upcoming sunset. After settling in, I looked at the happy faces of all the other guests that had congregated on the patio to watch the resort's evening sunset ritual. I might even have spotted the businesswoman from my flight, but like the change in countenance our group had experienced by being at the resort for five days, it was hard to match the uptight person I first saw on the plane with the relaxed woman standing at the end of the balcony.

We watched the yellow orb lowering toward the ocean, waiting for the moment when it kisses the water and turns all it touches into a beautiful orange-red (sometimes even green) line across the sky. It was pretty shocking just how much had happened since I watched a similarly magical moment happen that morning with the sunrise up on Haleakala. This time, instead of waiting to jump on a bike, it was time for another of the hotel's cultural offerings.

As dutifully recounted in the hotel release— and told to us by Clive at the luau—each day at sunset, a resort employee signals the end of the day by blowing a conch shell in the open-air lobby and then runs down the path toward the ocean, lighting the resort's decorative torches along the way. Once at the beach, the employee is joined by Clive, who offers a traditional Hawaiian chant to celebrate the day's passing. It sounded like a lovely ritual—even if it was something that Fred told me most of the resorts offered—and I wondered how I might replicate it in my mom's garden when I got home.

As I watched the sun setting and the ceremony commence, I got to thinking what an amazing turn of events had taken place for me to be sitting at this luxurious resort in Hawaii. I mean, here I was sipping a cocktail and watching the sunset from this side of the Pacific Ocean instead of 3,000 miles away combing through court documents and interviewing lawyers in Los Angeles.

"This," Fred said again (as if reading my mind), pointing to the drink and the sunset and everything else that surrounded us, "will keep you in this business."

I smiled and clinked glasses with him. "I think you just might be right, Fred."

"We travel writers might not make a lot of money, but we do get to live the life of those who do," he said.

"The people who make a lot of money don't live like this," Dorothy piped up from the other side of Fred, raising her own glass in a toast. "They're working all the time. This life is better."

She smiled. I smiled. Then, once the last tip of orange fell beneath the blue water and we heard the chant down at the beach, we turned our chairs back and saw that Philippa Chang had joined us. Philippa stood watching our happy faces looking out at the sunset and had a huge smile on her face as well. Yet again, she was impeccably dressed in another Hawaiian print dress, and I realized that the fact I noticed meant Mona was indeed rubbing off on me.

"I am so glad you are all enjoying the evening," Philippa said. "We have some tapas coming out for you shortly, but first I want to personally thank you all for coming and enjoying the Mokihana Resort & Spa."

She paused. "And, well, naturally I also need to apologize for Brandon—especially to you, Samantha. I, well, I mean we had no idea..."

"Oh my goodness. No need to apologize. How could you know?" I said. I mean, it wasn't her fault she hired a sociopath, right? That's what sociopaths do—sociopaths like Brandon and (to a lesser extent as he hadn't murdered anybody— that I knew of) Mr. Sports Copy Desk, who I knew right then and there was really in my past.

"Thank you," Philippa said. "You will all be glad to know that Frank is recovering well. He was just grazed in the shoulder by the bullet and didn't even need to stay in the hospital. He's convalescing at home, and we hope he will be back with us soon."

"Actually," a voice behind her said, "I couldn't help but come and wish you all a big farewell. I hope you will all come back and visit us again soon."

Philippa looked behind her and then stepped aside to reveal Frank, in the flesh, with a big ole sling over his right shoulder and that adorable smile on his face. As he waved (with his good arm), I noticed Frank pause as he looked over at Mac, who also had a big smile on his face, and wondered if they would be keeping in touch after the trip. I hoped so. They were just so darn cute together.

After another round of niceties, Philippa made sure Frank left to go home and recuperate. The rest of us sat and sipped our cocktails and tasted the tapas that had been brought out to the table. I will admit that Brandon had been right about one thing: The food we had at our opening reception was exactly the same as that in the restaurants and everywhere else in the resort. All of it was delicious. The biggest difference between tonight's meal and the first night's—except of course that Alistair had died, and Brandon was revealed to be a murderer—was that now I was the one with the story of adventure instead of listening to everyone else's.

"I still can't believe you rode Noe as a way to catch Brandon," Dorothy said.

"Too bad you never made it to Mama's Fish House," Fred said dryly.

"I wish we had been there to help you."

"So do I, Mac, so do I."

"Next time we're here, you'll have to show us that path under the zip line," Taylor said, smiling (yes, a real smile!).

As we all compared notes on our trips down the volcano, our other stops on the island, and what we had each discovered—not to mention more about the death of Alistair and Brandon's fall from grace (to say the least)—I looked around at their faces. They all were kind of glowing, both from the cocktails and our days in the Hawaiian sun. I realized felt a real kinship with each of them. Dorothy, Brian, Fred. Even Taylor had warmed and relaxed immensely and was laughing at something Mac said while Trevor took their picture and Brittany took a picture of him taking the picture.

For the first time, I was really starting to understand Mona's initial advice that it was like a Club Med without the sex, although in my mind it was more like the weeks of Girl Scout Camp my parents sent me off to every summer. Aside from the seasickness and harrowing horseback adventures, those had been some of the happiest moments of my childhood. I was out in the world meeting new people and really living life. That was something I thought I would find working as an investigative journalist, but it was so depressing only dealing with the darkest aspects of society. So, yeah, we had a murder, but otherwise, this week had been the most alive I felt in years.

I also realized that the time spent with this group of people sharing incredible experiences—experiences that, as Dorothy had astutely observed, most people never have a chance to—had created a bond that no one else was going to share. While I couldn't see my face, I'm going to guess I was glowing a bit, too.

After a while, the conversation started to wind down. Everyone had flights home the next day—some ridiculously early in the morning (thank god, not mine)—so it wasn't all that late before we exchanged cards and Instagram handles and gave each other a final hug, and I headed back to my room.

CHAPTER TWENTY

As I made my way down the hall to my room, there was something that compelled me to round the corner and continue walking down to look at Alistair's door (sorry, doors) again. With all that had gone on, I guess I was curious to see what it looked like. Did the aura of all that had transpired permeate from the well-appointed doors of his suite?

When I got there, I was surprised to find the door was open, and Detective Kai—Roger—was taking the police tape down.

"Well, well, what do we have here?" I said.

Roger turned and smiled, a real smile, a nice smile. "Sam, it's so good to see you."

"Are you still on duty?"

"Not technically. Most of the force is working a big car accident out on the Hana Highway, so

I said I would take care of this on my way home. This way the hotel can get in here and clean the room."

"Suite," we both said in unison and laughed.

There was a pause and then Roger added. "Kind of glad I did come by."

"Me, too." I'm not sure how big my smile was on the outside, but it was pretty darn big on the inside.

"Since the tape is down, and I am officially off duty, I would like to properly introduce myself. Hello, my name is Roger Kai," he said, offering his hand to shake.

"Nice to meet you, Roger. My name is Samantha Powers."

I took his hand and shook it. It felt good. Really good.

"Would you like to take a look?" he asked.

"Sure."

We both stepped into the suite and took a look around. The room looked spotless.

"In case you are wondering, the crime scene unit has already come to clean and bag everything that was left in here," he said.

I looked over at the bar area where the offending basket had been sitting. It also was clean as a whistle. "I see that. If we didn't know better, we'd never know anything had happened."

"Yeah, they do a good job at cleaning up," Roger said, still holding the yellow police tape in his hands as we looked out the living room windows toward the ocean.

"This suite really does have a beautiful verandah," I said.

Roger nodded, looked at his watch, and turned to look at me. "You know…" he said. "I told the hotel the suite would be available for them to come in and clean in an hour."

"An hour, huh. Well, you might be surprised to learn that the general manager had a lovely bottle of Veuve Clicquot delivered to each of our rooms. I'm not sure if it was an apology for Brandon or one last memorial to Alistair, but in either case, I can't take it in my carry-on and would hate for it to go to waste…"

"That would be a shame. I suppose in the interest of curbing wastefulness we could, you know, have a sip."

"And in that same interest, we wouldn't want to waste the final hour on this lovely verandah."

"We really wouldn't."

"Is it settled then?"

"It's settled."

I went and got the bottle from my room. When I came back, Roger had set up the ice bucket and two glasses out on the Molokini Suite's luxurious verandah—Alistair's verandah—the one he got by always asking for an upgrade, which I suppose was his biggest lesson to me in the short time we knew each other. Not that I ever thought I would become the type to ask for one, but learning to stand up for myself a little more wasn't necessarily a bad lesson to learn.

Roger and I sat in the lounge chairs and enjoyed the Veuve while looking out at the stars and enjoying the sound of the waves and the balmy air. The conversation flowed easily as we started getting to know each other as people and not detective and person-of-interest (or pain in the ass or whatever it is he saw me as before).

Roger told me about Maui—his Maui, growing up near Makawao as the son of two Haleakala park rangers and how although the name on his birth certificate (and on his badge) was Roger, everyone in his family called him Kula. Yes, the name of the town I had gone whizzing through on my bike. It was where they lived when he was born and means "open meadow." I thought it was fitting.

"Then maybe you can finally tell me about the bracelets, Kula."

He reflexively went to touch the four braided leather bands, which each had different symbols as clasps. "My sister makes them," he said. "She braids the leather and then creates the clasps out of bone to represent protection or accomplishments or hurdles that have been overcome."

Roger pointed to the bracelet with a fishhook clasp. "This makau—or fishhook—represents strength, prosperity, and good luck. Milanette gave it to me when I left to play volleyball at UC Santa Barbara."

"Nice. I went to UCLA."

"We played them a few times every year."

"Who knows? We might have crossed paths."

Roger smiled. "I like to think we did." Then he pointed to one that looked like a small lizard. "This gecko is known as a protector of homes, so she gave it to me when I got my first place on my own."

The next was a turtle. "This one is for the honu—green sea turtle—and symbolizes good luck and endurance. When lost, turtles are known as excellent navigators who are able to find their way home, so she made it for me when I came back from Iraq."

"I had a feeling you served in the military."

"Yeah, army intelligence. I enjoyed the work but wasn't happy with all the death that seemed to go along with it."

"I hear you. While nearly as dramatic as being in battle, covering crime in a big city like Los Angeles can be a little depressing," I said, then realized he was still involved in that world. "How is it now being a cop?"

"On an island like Maui, it's not too bad. We don't often get the Brandons of the world here, and even when we do, I feel like I'm doing my bit by serving as an advocate for the victims who no longer have a voice in this world."

"That's how my dad felt, too. But it can still wear on you."

"It can. But at least here in Maui, there is always the ocean to wash it off you."

"I thought you might be a surfer."

"Now and then. How did your dad wash it off?"

"I'm not sure he did," I said. "Except maybe with my mom and her garden. She was a florist."

"Was?"

"She died when I was in college."

"I'm sorry."

"Thank you," I said and then, realizing just how easy he was to talk to, just kept going. I told him about growing up in Carmel as the only child of two parents who met later in life. How hard communicating with my dad was, especially after my mom died, and even more since he got sick. How weird it was to be back home with my Uncle Henry and Buster (because, really, you can't talk about Carmel without talking about the dogs) and how I wasn't sure I wanted to go back to Los Angeles, especially now that my completely dysfunctional relationship was over. Yeah, I went there. Roger was just so easy to talk to, and obviously, I had been holding a LOT inside.

We talked about how our lives were changing now that we were in our 30s—especially mine with this new job. We both admitted we felt more formed as people but still were as confused as we ever were about what exactly our purpose in life was. You know? Roger did seem to know. It felt like the beginning of a real friendship—or perhaps something more (if the burgeoning butterflies in my gut were any clue)—was starting to form.

At a certain point—when I was talking about my mom—he reached his hand out and brushed it by mine. I felt like a teenager as I took it, and the butterflies went into overdrive. For the first time in a long time, I felt safe.

Unfortunately, as we both knew, time and geography were not on our side. I suppose in a way that is the tragedy—for lack of a better word—of travel. You meet the most wonderful people and then you leave them and don't know if you will ever see them again.

We were so lost in our conversation that when the knock and voice calling out "housekeeping" came, it was a surprise. Roger opened the door to Betty (from Kona) and told her he was with the police department and just finishing up but that she was welcome to start cleaning the suite. He bagged up the Veuve as I washed the glasses and left them to dry next to the sink.

We told Betty we were leaving, and he walked me the long seven rooms back to my room. We paused in front, and I sublimated my desire to jump into his arms and drag him inside. Instead, we enjoyed a lingering hug. Then, he took one of the bracelets off his wrist. The clasp was in the shape of a spiral.

"I want you to have this, Sam. This is a koru, which comes from the Maori name for a coil or loop, like those found in the fern sprouts that grow there. It is used here to represent a new beginning in the circle of life. I think that is where you are, Sam. A new beginning."

He placed the bracelet onto my wrist and then looked into my eyes and gave me a tender kiss that made my knees buckle. "You are pretty amazing, Samantha Powers. I can't wait to see what you do next."

I'm not sure how he knew just how much that I needed to hear that with all I'd been through in the past year, but for the first time, I was looking to the future without apprehension.

"Thank you, Roger Kai. You're pretty amazing yourself."

We talked about keeping in touch and meeting up if either of us was able to get to each other's towns—who knows? It might happen. (Heck, I might have to come and testify in Brandon's trial.) Either way, I went to bed with a smile on my face.

CHAPTER
TWENTY-ONE

The next morning, Brittany was at my door—literally standing right outside it—to make sure I was ready to head to the airport at the appointed time. I was flying through Los Angeles, where Brittany was based, to Monterey so she had scheduled our flights at the same time to make sure I made it at least to California without any other "adventures." I assured her that I was fine and that I loved the resort and that the readers of *Carmel Today* didn't need to know about the murder in the Molokini Suite or the resort's crazed former director of sales.

That got me to thinking about what exactly I was going to write. The words started forming in my head as the plane took off, and I looked from my window seat out onto the lush landscape, swaying palm trees, and blue ocean framing the airport in Kahului, Maui. As I fiddled with the bracelet on my wrist, it occurred to me that while resorts with ridiculously large TVs, orchids, white duvets, and heated toilet seats were lovely (really, really lovely), it was the people who provided the true riches. People like Philippa, with her elegance and eye for detail; Simone, who remembered my smoothie every day; Margaret, the housekeeper who left the daily notes on my bed; and even Frank, happily taking me on the bike ride down a path Elua found to make guests feel special.

The plane took off toward the east. I looked down and spotted the road that led up to Haleakala and saw where it came together with the road to Hana near the ocean. I then followed the Hana Highway along the coastline until I saw the entrance to the zipline with the wires suspended over the gulch just above it. From there, I found the patches of jungle opening occasionally into the small paths that led to a cattle ranch, a glorious artist's compound, and a gorgeous waterfall that spilled into the gulch and down toward the sea. Looking down at the scene of so many of my adventures on the island, I realized that the true riches of Maui didn't stop at the resort's edge. There, too, it was the people that made it special: from Kekoa and Grant, my stoic heroes, to Roger, with his warm and intelligent eyes. And, okay, Noe was pretty special, too. As I laid my head back into my chair, I thought about the words I would use to describe what I was feeling.

As service-oriented as the staff members at the Mokihana Resort & Spa are—and they truly are— the level of hospitality they provide is not something felt just within the property but a characteristic found throughout the island of Maui. It is in the people that one finds the true spirit of Aloha, a spirit that envelops the visitor—especially those who are respectful of the local culture—and, when added to scenery that makes the heart sing, creates a longing to return. And isn't that the true meaning of paradise?

I was so inspired I pulled out my laptop and wrote most of the story—1,000 scintillating words, as assigned—on the plane ride home. Every activity I described brought a smile to my face that stayed there pretty much the whole two flights home. Before I knew it, the wheels were hitting the ground at Monterey Regional Airport.

I walked through the small terminal and out to the curb. Uncle Henry was teaching a class and Lizzy was working at the Paws Up, so while it wasn't a surprise that no one was there to greet me at the airport, it was perhaps a bit of a shock to the system. Hello? Where was the Monterey County equivalent of the Hawaiian hunk placing a fragrant lei over to my head while my luggage was being whisked into a luxury SUV? Instead, I called a rideshare and rode the short 20-minute ride back to the house.

Once there, I dropped my bags in my room before heading down to the main house. I did my usual walk out onto the garden patio that overlooked the beach. It was hard to believe that I had just come from across the same ocean. Across all that water was the resort, not to mention Frank and Philippa, Noe and Kekoa—and Roger. I looked around and had a new appreciation of what we had here in Carmel—what my great grandparents, grandparents, and parents had all built. I realized that even without all the little niceties from the Mokihana Resort & Spa (I would have to talk to Uncle Henry to gauge his thoughts about adding heated toilet seats and lighting torches at sunset), it was a pretty nice place to be.

The next day at the *Carmel Today* offices, I went over all the photos I took with Ben, the production designer, gave the story a final edit, and turned it into Mona. Later, as I was leaving for the day, FU Chelsea was proofing the next issue and asked me to weigh in on another argument she was having with Toupee Tom.

"I just don't think some people will know what a 'cap' is," (yes, she used the quote marks) Chelsea said with a smirk. Really, it was a smirk. "Perhaps we should call it a 'baseball hat.'"

"But, but, it is not a hat at all," said Tom, his pale complexion starting to turn pink with anger.

"If it isn't clear to the editor, it won't be clear to the reader," Chelsea parroted in her most annoying tone.

"Our readers are not imbeciles, Chelsea."

"Sam, help me out here," Chelsea said, looking over at me as if we were on the same team.

"Yeah, Chelsea, that's not going to happen," I said. "Tom is right. Tom is always right."

On Chelsea's peeved (to say the least) look, I winked at Tom and walked out the door and over to Lizzy's cafe. Uncle Henry was there waiting to hand off Buster as I had a dad visit planned after I said hello to everyone. I was surprised to find Mona (with Cornwall, of course) already there and even more surprised to find Diego sitting at the end of the bar. His rescue greyhound Ellie was sleeping at his feet next to Canoodle, Beth's dog. Yep, I was back in dogville. Really, Noe would have been perfectly at home, don't you think? I joined the group up at the bar while the four pooches enjoyed their social time at our feet.

"Oh good, you're here," Lizzy said. "Henry's just finishing reading us your story."

I looked over at Mona and she shrugged. "I thought they should see just what an evocative travel writer you are, Samantha."

"*And isn't that the true meaning of paradise?*" Uncle Henry said, putting the pages down. "Nice. I like how you managed to work in everything you did without mentioning the murder."

"Thanks," I said. "Mona, naturally, had a say in that."

"Mundane things like murder have no place in the *Carmel Today* lifestyle," Mona said with a smile as Cornwall yakked something he'd just eaten up onto the floor. "Cornwall!"

"No worries, I got it," Lizzy said, pulling out her ever-present dustpan and mop.

"Congratulations, Sam," Diego said, looking me in the eye for the first time since I'd returned. "Really good story. I'm glad you're safely home."

"Thank you," I said. "And I mean, really, thank you."

I gave Diego a smile and he smiled in return. I hoped that maybe we were moving past the weirdness of our encounter (for lack of a better word) and toward a new friendship. Seeing him again though, I have to say, reminded me just how good-looking he was. Tall, dark, and handsome Diego. Damn. I inadvertently touched the bracelet Roger had given me and was reminded we had a video chat scheduled for later that night.

"I notice you didn't mention the path you took through Grant Willoughby's compound— or even seeing him," Uncle Henry said, thankfully turning everyone's attention away from Diego and me.

"Who's that?" Lizzy asked.

"Sam didn't tell you about him? Grant Willoughby is an artist. He's huge. They just had a retrospective of his last year at the Museum of Modern Art in San Francisco, but nobody has seen him in person in years."

216

Again, I smiled. "There are some things a travel writer does not reveal."

"She said it. You heard her!" Mona said.

"I did indeed," Lizzy said.

Okay, so yeah, I guess I was now officially a travel writer.

After a drink with the gang, I took Buster and walked back over to Ocean Avenue. We headed down past the restaurants and shops and galleries and wine tasting rooms before turning on the side street that led to the assisted living center. There I would have my first visit with my dad after getting back. After making our way through the old-lady puppy-voice gauntlet, Buster and I sat next to my dad at his table. He did his usual scrutinizing of me like I was one of his suspects. Then, when I could see the realization as to who it was he was talking to hit, he started with his usual question: "Following a case?"

"You know, I was, Dad. I was."

I told him about traveling to Maui to write about the Mokihana Resort & Spa, the death of Alistair, and everything else that ensued—including the fact I actually rode a horse without being rubbed off on a tree and got to check out the Maui police station (I may have left out why) and how I was, you know, pretty darn helpful in bringing the killer to justice.

"Was it the wife?"

"Not this time, Dad. Not this time."

He got a surprised look, so I filled him in on how I found the picture with the teeth that gave the director of sales away as the killer. Then I segued to the gorgeous suite I found it in and the beautiful room I got to stay in at the resort with its view of the ocean and palm trees. I told him how much I loved the feel of the warm breeze and the sounds of the birds and the smell of the flowers—even the flowers that were used as the murder weapon.

As I continued to tell the story, I got a response I hadn't seen in him in a long time. He smiled, and for a moment, it was like I could see through those piercing blue eyes of his back into a brain that was still working even if it wasn't able to communicate all of its machinations to me. Then he said something that really surprised me because we never NEVER discussed feelings, even—or especially—when it came to my mom.

"You know, your mom loved Hawaii."

"I know she did, Dad."

"We went there on our honeymoon."

"I remember you two talking about it."

"She especially liked all the flowers."

"I know she did, Dad."

"A lot of them we can't grow here. Too cold. But she tried, you know. She did try." Then his face brightened with another memory. "We brought home a seedling... Picked it up at a nursery. I can't remember the name of, you know, the thing..."

"It was probably a plumeria, Dad."

"Yes! That is what it was. We brought it home, but it didn't like the cool weather."

"That's what you said."

Then he brightened. "But I think your mom might have made one work in the greenhouse at the shop, though. Yes, I think she did."

"I'll check it out with the new owners next time I'm out that way, Dad."

"That would be good." He smiled—and it wasn't the interrogation smile, either. Then, after a moment, the smile faded, and he looked at me again, as if just realizing who was sitting next to him. "So. You're home."

"Yep. I'm home."

"Why?"

"For you, Dad."

"I don't need your help."

"Ya kinda do, Dad."

"What will you do?"

"I'm a travel writer now. Working for Mona at *Carmel Today*."

"Oh. Okay. That's nice. Good luck with that."

The smile returned as did the glimmer in the back of his blue eyes. "Yeah, good luck with that."

Then he noticed Buster sitting beside me. "Buster!"

THE END

About
the Author

In her 20+ years as a writer and editor, Ann Shepphird has covered everything from travel and sports to gardening and food to design and transportation for a variety of publications.

Now Ann is tackling her favorite topics— mysteries and rom-coms—for 4 Horsemen Publications. The Destination Murder mysteries combine Ann's experiences as a travel journalist with her stint working for a private investigator, while the University Chronicles series of rom-coms are based on Ann's days as a college-level communications instructor.

Ann lives in Santa Monica, California, with her long-time partner, Jeff, and their furry companions Melody and Winnie. When she's not writing, Ann is most likely to be found on a tennis court or in her garden.

Discover More...

annshepphird.com

facebook.com/authorannshepphird

Instagram: @ashepphird

Twitter: @ashepphird

ashepphird@gmail.com

Books...

The War Council

Destination: Maui,
a Destination Murder Mystery

Destination: Monterey,
a Destination Murder Mystery

4 Horsemen Publications

Romance

Emily Bunney
All or Nothing
All the Way
All Night Long
All She Needs
Having it All
All at Once
All Together
All for Her

Lynn Chantale
The Baker's Touch
Blind Secrets

Mimi Francis
Private Lives
Second Chances
Run Away Home
The Professor

4HorsemenPublications.com

CPSIA information can be obtained
at www.ICGtesting.com
Printed in the USA
BVHW071052120122
625988BV00008B/707